Christmas: A Season for Angels

Bedside Books
An imprint of American Book Publishing
5442 So. 900 East, #146
Salt Lake City, UT 84117-7204
www.american-book.com
Printed in the United States of America on acid-free paper.

Christmas: A Season for Angels

Designed by Jana Rade, design@american-book.com

Publisher's Note: *This is a work of fiction. Names, characters, places, and incidents either are the product of the author's imagination, or are used fictitiously, and any resemblance to actual persons, living or dead, events, or locales is entirely coincidental.*

ISBN-13: 978-1-58982-496-6
ISBN-10: 1-58982-496-2

Julian, Vicki L., Christmas: A Season for Angels

Special Sales

These books are available at special discounts for bulk purchases. Special editions, including personalized covers, excerpts of existing books, and corporate imprints, can be created in large quantities for special needs. For more information e-mail info@american-book.com.

Christmas: A Season for Angels

By

Vicki L. Julian

To the memory of my late husband, Steve, who was many times my angel on earth.

CONTENTS

Foreword	9
Preface	11
Introduction	13
Ruth	15
Jennifer	25
Brad	35
Mike	47
Marsha	53
Ryan	61
Jill	71
Robert	81
Christopher	95
Leah	107
Conclusion	115
Acknowledgments	117
About the Author	119

FOREWORD

What do such diverse literary greats as Isaac Asimov, Ray Bradbury, John Cheever, Paul Gallico, Edgar Allen Poe, John Steinbeck and Mark Twain have in common? They all, from time to time, have been inspired to use angels as a source of inspiration in their writings.

And those authors are not alone in their fascination with angels. Studies indicate that most Americans believe in angels and a 2005 Harris poll shows that sixty eight percent of Americans believe in angels, while seventeen percent do not and fifteen percent are not sure if angels exist. Respondents were not polled on whether they wanted to believe in angels or hoped they are real.

In her collection of fictional stories about angels — both in Celestial and human form — Vicki Julian provides insight into the everyday angels who may be at work in our own lives.

—Marsha Henry Goff, freelance writer, columnist

PREFACE

This book was born in 2007 out of my need for comfort as I faced the second Christmas without my soul mate, best friend, and husband. One night I decided to go upstairs to my computer, expecting to journal or to write a letter to my late husband as I had done many times before. Instead, I found myself writing the first of these ten stories.

Although I have written many things in my life, it always took my concentrated effort and organization to make the work flow, and to create a plausible ending. This first story and those that followed truly felt as though they were written through me rather than by me. There was no thought to what direction they would take, or how they would end. They seemed to write themselves. The process was always the same; sit down, begin writing, and three hours later, the story was complete.

Some of the characters are loosely based on family and friends, and in retrospect are what I, too, think God would give them as comfort. In fact, I'm fairly certain of that because, again, I had no idea where the stories were going or how they would end. Divinity intervened. Other stories in this book have no particular basis; however, I felt the characters very strongly. In each case, the individuals in every story are very real to me. They are God's people in need of comfort.

Although I am a Christian and a believer, no one is more surprised than I about being a Christian author. I am not a zealot or someone who can easily recite Biblical passages, but in writing this book, God brought healing to me. My hope is that this book will also bring comfort, peace, hope, and entertainment to others with the simple message that God cares.

May angels watch over you to answer your prayers at Christmas and always.

INTRODUCTION

Angels can be seen or unseen. They can be messengers, protectors, guides, or even answers to a prayer. They can also be ethereal or human because God can work through real angels or bestow upon us an angelic task to do His will.

Some of the best angel interventions come at Christmas because it is a holy and magical time where believers and nonbelievers alike are touched. During this sacred and celebratory season of Jesus' birth, many life-changing events are said to occur. This is the time when prayers are answered, and the desires of all mankind can be met. Good tidings are shared, love overflows, and the community of man, believers and nonbelievers, realizes its shared humanity.

At Christmas, God hears the plight of His children and sends an angel to fulfill His promise that He will watch over and care for us. Whether the angel is ethereal or human, rest assured, all are Heaven sent. It is a time when "believe, and all things are possible" is more than recitation. It is truth. These are the stories of those who have witnessed that truth.

RUTH

She didn't drive anymore; it was simply no longer a choice. Her eyesight had been progressively failing for the last twenty years, but, in truth, she simply had not aged well since losing her husband. It had been fifteen years since she lost Henry, her best friend, her lover, her life companion. They had been inseparable since they had first met in their late teens. Later, she was a beautiful young bride of twenty, and he a handsome young gent of twenty-one when they married. Together, dreams had always been very much a part of their lives, even into their seventies. Travelling, sharing in the good deeds of serving others, enjoying concerts and plays, and of course, just sitting quietly next to each other immersed in private thoughts. When Henry passed on, all of her dreams died too. At ninety-two, she had no desire other than to be with her darling Henry.

It was cold outside and looking a lot like snow. Ruth shivered at the thought of being housebound for months on end again. She was fragile. She depended on the goodness of organizations for much of her needs, whether to the drug store for medicines, doctor visits or for purchasing groceries. Had she not been able to sit in the swing on her patio during the more pleasant weather days, she would have felt claustrophobic year-round.

She pushed aside the thought of isolation once again and made herself a cup of green tea. That is something she and Henry always enjoyed together. They thought it was healthful even before science said it was, and given their many years together, it did prove to be very good for them. Add an oatmeal cookie and it was a perfect afternoon snack.

What also crept into her thoughts was that the "season" was coming up. There would be Thanksgiving and then Christmas; just two more big days during which she would go into her own world and miss Henry. Oh, there was the Thanksgiving dinner at the church to which other church members would transport her, but there was also the vast loneliness. She could not go many places like others and it was so difficult just to get up in the morning and dress. It seemed that each day it was getting a little harder to greet life.

She and Henry had not been able to have children although they interacted with children whenever they could. After Ruth retired from teaching and Henry from farming, they taught Sunday school to four- and five-year-olds. They also volunteered for "grandparent" activities at the local elementary schools, and played "grandpa" and "grandma" to generations of neighborhood children. But much of that ended when Henry died. She had tried to remain cheerful and helpful, but eventually failing health and lack of *joie de vive* left her with little desire to do the things she once did.

As she sat nursing her tea, tears flowed and she began to pray.

"Dear God, I am so lonely without my Henry. I have no real friends, only acquaintances. If I must spend my days on this earth, please make my Christmas not so sad. Let me spend it with people who will help me see my life as something good. I don't want to spend this Christmas alone, God."

As she finished the prayer, her eyes welled with tears again. She remembered so many Christmases that she spent alone in the past, maybe seeing someone drop by for fifteen minutes to bring some Christmas goodies and dinner, and maybe a small gift. But how many lacy handkerchiefs or scarves does one need over the years? It's not that she wasn't grateful; what she really needed was companionship. She needed someone to talk to and to share. She needed to be loved.

When she had finished the last drop of tea, Ruth placed her head in both hands and began to sob, finally resting all on the table. Soon, a deep exhaustion overcame her and she began to doze. In this twilight moment, between wakefulness and sleep, she heard a knock on the door. She rose from the table and glanced at the clock. It was 3:30 p.m. and she certainly was not expecting anyone. She peered through the peep hole and saw a woman standing outside the door. She opened it a crack and said, "Yes?"

"May I come in?" the woman asked.

Gazing at the stranger from head to toe, Ruth decided the woman looked harmless enough. She opened the door and responded, "Please."

"I'm your Christmas angel, Ruth, but you can call me Merry."

Ruth's first thought was that she had just allowed a crazy person to enter her home. But something in the woman's gaze was both gentle and kind, and Ruth felt immediately at ease. Merry's expression just made her feel comfortable and safe.

"I'm here because of your prayer."

"My prayer?" gasped Ruth. "You heard my prayer?"

"I didn't, but God did," answered Merry.

At this revelation, Ruth stumbled backward and sat on her dainty sofa. It was the one she and Henry had purchased nearly half-a-century ago. Sensing that Ruth was trying to process what she had just heard, Merry sat next to her on the sofa and gently reached for her hand.

"Ruth, God knows that you have been lonely since you lost Henry, and He also knows that you have been a good and faithful servant when you could do so. He has chosen to answer your prayer through me."

Looking into her eyes, Ruth asked, "You're going to spend Christmas with me? I'm not going to be alone this year?"

Merry smiled. "In answer to your first question, technically, no. But I am going to see that your prayer is answered. You will not be lonely this year."

"But how then?" Ruth quizzed.

"Just leave that to me. Spend Thanksgiving as you wish and prepare for Christmas as always."

She then placed her hand beside Ruth's cheek to give a comforting touch and then rose.

With her heart a little less heavy, Ruth gazed at the angel with wonder. Merry was beautiful. Her stature, long and trim, complemented a regal countenance. She had long wavy brown hair, green eyes and a fair complexion, but it was the kindness emanating from her that embodied her true beauty. It was the angel's soul that she truly saw. And then it occurred to Ruth that Merry was different now than when she had first entered her home. There was no overcoat, hat, scarf or boots.

She now wore a to-the-floor white gown with lace and pearls adorning the bodice. The full skirt flowed in cascades of silken material and a halo of light encircled her head. Just beyond her shoulders, Ruth could see the feathery billows of wings. They stared at each other for a brief moment and Merry evaporated before Ruth's watchful gaze.

Suddenly Ruth opened her eyes and her head began to swim. *Did I just have the strangest dream?* she wondered. *Or could it maybe have been real? Let's see. I had my tea. I cried, but I know that I dozed,* she remembered. *But I feel so warm, so comforted, like it had to be real. Maybe God did hear my prayer and He won't let me be lonely this Christmas. Yes,* she conceded, *I know it with all my heart.*

For the first time in a long while, Ruth gave a little smile and felt a little joy creeping back into her heart. She had always loved Christmas, but felt bad that she could not enjoy the season as she had when Henry was alive. She knew that her Lord's birthday was certainly reason for celebration. After all, His coming into the world was why she knew she would spend eternity with her Henry. It was just that the separation here on earth seemed so long and empty.

During the next week, Ruth made plans for Thanksgiving. This year she had something in the future for which to be thankful, and she felt the desire to share. She made the list of groceries she would need so that the volunteer sent by the senior citizen's group could shop for her. She wanted to take something to the church's community Thanksgiving dinner this year; the sweet potato pie that she once made. Yes, the pie that everyone loved and for which she received brief and appreciative fame some years ago.

The Wednesday before Thanksgiving, she received her expected call from the church members who would escort her to the dinner. This year, it was the Fredricksens. They were nice people, she remembered. They had one daughter who was abroad studying in England. She felt sorry that their daughter must not be coming back for Thanksgiving, but maybe she would be here for Christmas. *I'll say a little prayer for them,* she thought. *After all, I know that God does answer prayers. Well,* she hesitated, *maybe He hasn't actually answered mine yet, but Merry told me that He will.* And she smiled again.

Later that afternoon, her pie came out of the oven perfectly done. She cooled it and then set it in the refrigerator for the night. Tomorrow, she would let it reach room temperature before it was served to those fortunate enough to "win" a piece. That night, she slept well and remembered to thank God again for the special gift He would give her for Christmas.

The Fredricksens picked her up at eleven in the morning, promptly as scheduled, and she enjoyed each of the three hours spent at the church dinner. She was tired when she returned home. These outings took so much of her energy, but this time it was worth every ounce she could muster. Her last thoughts that evening were that she would try to set up her little tree tomorrow, but tonight would be peaceful.

Ruth greeted each of the next few weeks with growing expectation. *How will I know who will spend Christmas with me? What should I get to give them as a present? When will I know?* She finally wondered with exasperation.

As it grew closer to Christmas, Ruth tried hard to maintain her cheerful demeanor. It was difficult to be alone and have very few contacts with whom to share the season. Her lowest point was on the 23rd of December. She began to question whether the anticipated answer to her prayer was real. *Maybe it was just a silly dream after all,* she thought. And as quickly as her eyes began to well with tears, peace overcame her. She sat back, closed her eyes and let the feeling envelop her. Yes, it was true. Her prayer would be answered. God had sent Merry, her Christmas angel, to assure her of that. Even if it was in a dream, it was still a vision.

It was snowing when she woke up on the 24th. It must have started during the night because there were three inches on her stoop by nine in the morning. *How will my guests come if it snows too much?* she worried. Then, just as quickly she remembered that all things are possible with God.

She prepared her usual egg, toast, and tea and then sat on her sofa to watch the twinkling lights on her tree. She eyed the wrapped box of chocolates under the tree that she purchased for the unknown guests who would be spending Christmas with her. That seemed like an appropriate gift. Any gender and any age could surely enjoy the box of chocolates. And, in the back of her mind, she thought that she, too, would enjoy them if something in her promise of prayer fulfillment fell through. She again fought with any doubt and tried to focus on the beautiful little tree.

The rest of the afternoon and evening were uneventful. No calls, no cards in the mail, no one sharing the season of love with her. As she slipped into bed, she fought tears again and tried hard to remember that her answered prayer would be not to spend Christmas alone. *I know God promised,* she repeated to herself over and over, *and He does not lie. Merry told me that He heard me and would answer my prayer. I will not be alone this year!* With a self-assured final sigh, she drifted into a comfortable slumber. As the grandfather clock began to toll the midnight hour, Ruth stirred slightly. She briefly gained semi-consciousness and saw that Merry was standing next to her bed.

"I knew you were real," she whispered. After a pause, she added, "I thought you weren't going to spend Christmas with me."

"I'm not," answered the angel. "I'm here to take you to Heaven. This year you will spend Christmas with those you love and who love you. Come and take my hand, Ruth. Henry is waiting."

The next day, Gwen Samuel knocked on the door of Ruth's little house. There was nothing to indicate the stirring of any creature or soul. It was one o'clock that afternoon and Gwen had the customary treats and small gift. When her attempts to rouse someone failed, she thought, *Hmmmm. Someone must have come and taken Ruth to spend Christmas elsewhere this year.* It was another forty years when Gwen finally reached Heaven before she knew how right she had been.

JENNIFER

Twenty-six with a small child, no husband, dead-end job, but breathing. Jennifer sighed as she mentally concocted a response to an online dating service. She closed her eyes and thought, *That's my life in a nutshell. Sounds interesting? Even I wouldn't date me!* she concluded.

Thoughts also entered her mind that it wouldn't be long before Emily awakened from her nap. "Oh, God," she half prayed. "I hate my life. If I didn't have Emily, I'd just shrivel up and die. It's too hard, God. Give me someone to love and this time, make sure that it's returned."

Huh, she mused while straightening up in the chair. *Let's see if God can give me the right words to make that happen.* "Single mother wishes to meet knight in shining armor who can rescue her and her daughter from the dumps," she typed. *Nope, that's not going to do it! How desperate do you have to be to do online dating anyway?* And with that she pushed the keyboard under the desk and closed the online dating form. Turning away from the computer and getting up, she crossed the room to the small kitchen.

After making herself a cup of hot cocoa, she decided to curl up with a good romance novel and just read until Emily awoke. Two paragraphs in, the phone rang. It was Jane Cuthelbert, her personal blind date fixer-upper. Jane meant well, but Jennifer couldn't help thinking of all the dates that Jane thought would be a great match, but there was no flame. She chuckled to herself at the little joke she had just made.

"We're having a Christmas open house on the 12th and we want you to come."

"Oh no, Jane, not another setup, please," Jennifer begged.

"No, dear friend, it's just an open house so don't get your hopes up or your feathers ruffled. Besides," Jane admonished, "you haven't been too kind to the last dates I fixed you up with."

"So you've finally given up on me, huh?" she half mused, but with a sigh of relief.

"Well, not really," Jane confessed. "It's just that I can't find anybody in your age group who is available that night. It seems that we aren't the only party in town. But come anyway. I do have one single male and a whole bunch of competition for him. He's way too old for you so you don't have to feel threatened. I won't make you go out with *him*," she laughed.

"Well, in that case, OK. What time, so I know when to get a babysitter?" And with that, Jennifer was unknowingly on her way to meeting Mr. Right.

Five days passed and d-day had finally arrived. Jennifer awoke with a groggy head. *Too many romance novels,* she sighed. *And I've got to stop reading till two in the morning!* Emily would soon be awake and then it would be a busy day.

She thought about the online dating service again, but decided that she really didn't want to do that until after the new year. *Get a new start, try something different, reinvent the ol' Jennifer,* she concluded. Her mind then drifted to tonight. *Now what do I wear to an open house party when I don't have to look desirable? Ha! Anything I darn well please!* With that she chose a cute little red sweater with sparkles and black pants. Add her Christmas reindeer socks and she would be *open-house, don't-care-if-I-meet-anybody, perfect!*

The day was spent doing a little Christmas baking, cookies that she and Emily would freeze and take to her parents' house on Christmas day; a brief shopping excursion where she purchased a small hostess gift for tonight; cleaning the house and decorating the fridge with more of Emily's preschool drawings of the season.

When she finally dropped Emily off at the sitter's, she was having second thoughts about going to the open house. *What I'd really like to do is just go home and take a nap,* but she knew that was not going to happen. Accept an invitation and you have to go. That's what her mother had drilled into her.

She remembered when she had accepted an invitation to prom with Derek Janks and decided that he was too much of a dweeb to go with. Her mother found out that she was trying to break the date a week before the event, and that erupted into a true battle of wills. In the end, she took her mother's advice and didn't have an altogether bad time. *Well, she rationalized, Jane and David's open house would be more fun since she at least liked them. And, thankfully Jane isn't trying to set me up this time!*

She walked up to the door and was greeted by some cheery little reindeer in the wreath that hung upon it. "Merry Christmas!" it announced. *Yeah, right,* she thought.

Hearing Rudy Reindeer give his greeting, Jane waltzed to the door and opened it. Before she could say anything, Jane blurted, "You look lovely! Come on in."

It was apparent to Jennifer that Jane had been at the eggnog or wassail bowl a little too long.

"This is for you," Jennifer said while handing over the hostess gift as she stepped inside.

"There are some people I want you to meet," Jane announced, "but I think you know most everyone. A lot are from church. You know, the usual group; the Sandersons, Bilks, Groenings, Salks, and Beatrice Smith, Dolly Ames, Joyce Bleethe." Grabbing Jennifer by the hand, she tried to introduce her to anyone she might not know. Finally, it occurred to Jane that she hadn't offered anything to Jennifer. She pointed toward the other end of the room where there was a large table with buffet items. Near to that was a table with eggnog and wassail.

"Help yourself, Jen." And with that, Jane was off on another venture.

Jennifer walked toward the tables while giving her pleasant I'm-happy-to-be-here-smile, really...As she picked up one of the plastic plates, a very nice-looking and spry older man stepped beside her.

"Ah, what's a nice girl like you doing in a place like this?" he cooed and then laughed.

"Wow, is that ever an old one!" she laughed back. "My name's Jennifer." Extending her hand, she noticed that he was fairly tall, slender, white-haired with only a little balding, but with some of the bluest and kindest eyes she had ever seen. And they sparkled!

"I'm Stan," he said, taking her hand. "So how do you know the Cuthelberts and how did they blackmail a cute young thing like you into coming?"

"Hmmmm," she started. "It's really quite a long story because we go back quite a way, but I'll give you the condensed version." And she smiled again thinking of how her friendship with them had blossomed over the years.

"I actually met Jane while grocery shopping one day after I moved into the area. My baby was causing all kinds of problems while I was trying to bag my groceries and Jane came over and offered to help. We began talking and she started inviting me places. I went to her church a few times. I was kind of at the lowest part of my life and I really needed a friend. The only problem is that she keeps trying to set me up with men who aren't exactly my cup of tea."

"Ahhh, that's one of Jane's foibles," Stan said, "but we love her anyway. She does that to me, too."

During the rest of the evening, they spent a great deal of time talking, much to the chagrin of the older ladies present. It appeared that she and Stan had much in common, but it was also apparent that their ages did not make them love interests, either. After the party, Jennifer mused, *Well, I guess God must have answered my prayers for Christmas. I should have been clear that I wasn't just looking for platonic friendship love.* But on the other hand, Jennifer felt herself strangely satisfied. She and Stan decided to meet for tea and go shopping on Saturday. She could get Stan to watch Emily while she slipped some items unseen into her cart. Emily was still too young to understand that the cart held wonderful surprises.

After the shopping spree, the three had dinner together and Jennifer caught herself thinking, *It's too bad that he's too old for me.* Then, just as quickly, she thought, *Oh my God. I am thinking of him as a love interest!* That also quickly brought her into the present. *No, just a friend,* she decided.

Stan was explaining how sad he had been since losing his wife eighteen months earlier.

"She was the light of my life. We did everything together, and until she got sick three years ago, we had a really great life."

He went on to talk about his daughter and son who lived two states away and across the country respectively.

"You don't have any family in this area?" she asked.

"My sister and her family live about an hour away. I see them sometimes. I'll probably go there for Christmas. My kids have in-law stuff this year. They try to alternate with me, but my daughter's husband just lost his mother this past year and they need to be with her father-in-law. I can understand. I've been there. So what are you going to do?"

"We're planning on going to my parents' house," Jennifer responded. "They live nearby and my sister and her family will also be there."

And so began the first of their intimate conversations that would signal their close relationship. Over the next ten days, they checked on each other via phone and occasionally provided the companionship that each so wanted. And then it was finally Christmas.

What a great friendship, Jennifer thought as she was preparing to go to her parents' house. *I need to drop off this small gift for Stan on the way.* And later as she was driving up to his house, she noticed an unfamiliar car in the driveway. *That's strange.* Then another thought occurred to her, a pang of fear.

What if something's happened to Stan? He was supposed to go somewhere, not have company!

Her first impulse was to run to the door, but she remembered Emily was asleep in the backseat. She quickly unbuckled her daughter from the child car seat and raced to the door. "Oh, dear God, you answered my prayer for Christmas and sent Stan to me. Please let him be OK." Just then the door opened and a handsome young man in his late twenties opened the door. "You must be Jennifer."

"Yes," she managed to say. "Is Stan all right?"
"He's fine. I'm Joel, his great-nephew. My uncle has been talking about you nonstop. He also said that I needed to meet you. I just decided to drive up here and get Stan since he would have to drive in some unfamiliar territory. My grandparents recently moved and Stan hasn't been there yet. I thought I would just acquaint him with the route first."

Realizing that there was no cause for alarm, Jennifer looked at Joel again as for the first time. Shockingly, he was handsome! He even looked a little like a younger version of Stan with his slender and tall stature, dark hair and wonderfully blue and kind eyes! *No ring on his finger, either,* she noticed.

*He already knows about me, knows I have a child…*thought Jennifer.

Suddenly, Stan appeared at the door. "Well, let her in, Joel," he admonished. "It's cold outside and we have to exchange gifts."

Stan didn't realize it, but he had just given Jennifer the gift that she had really prayed for. He was her Christmas angel.

BRAD

Brad was an advertising genius. As the chief executive of his company, he enjoyed a large home, business perks, financial security, and an appreciative family. At least that was the case nine months ago, until the fateful day when his company went bankrupt and everything had to be sold to satisfy debts and investors. His wife of twenty years could not handle the shame and left two months later. Their daughter and son, both teenagers, left with her. Not wishing to explain things to their friends anymore, the three left in the middle of the night.

How do things like this happen to a forty-eight-year-old man? he wondered. His rise had been stellar and he had owned his company since he was thirty-six. Twenty-three years of building a perfect life, and everything was gone in what seemed to be an instant. Brad had been poor growing up as the son of a proud and hard-working African-American custodian, but it was different now. Then he could only guess at what he didn't have. Now, he knew.

It was humiliating and humbling to realize that he had both attained and then lost the American dream. A black man's rise to the top. A beautiful wife and handsome children. People respected him and, most importantly to Brad, they envied him. As with many persons who are well-to-do, he had used some of his wealth for good and noble causes. He attended church and mentored young people of color who aspired to his status in life. He could give just a small portion of his enormous wealth and it seemed so much to others. They had no idea that his $10,000 contribution to this cause or that was only a mere fraction of his monthly salary. But he was comforted in knowing that he was still doing good, and much more than most people could do.

As Brad sat on the curb outside the place of his latest employment rejection, he put his head in his hands and gently stroked his throbbing temples. *Thank God my parents aren't alive to see me like this,* he thought. *And my kids. Oh, Lord, my kids. Thank God Teresa's sister was able to take them in.*

Then out of nowhere, he realized an overwhelming desire to pray.

"Oh, God. I can't seem to find a break. I'm lost and I'm scared. I miss my family. It's just two weeks to Christmas and I have no job. Unemployment means I can't eat more than one meal a day and I can't make ends meet. I want to send my kids something for Christmas and tell my wife how sorry I am. I'm desperate, Lord. I need a job. I need meaning in my life. Help me, please."

He sat there for another four or five minutes and realized that it had started to rain. Just as a car whizzed past, spraying water off the windshield, Brad realized that he needed to go home. To his one-bedroom apartment with second-hand stick furniture. It wasn't great, but at least it would be out of the rain. And there was one more can of beans for supper. He had to keep up his strength. Already, his once finely tailored suits hung on his emaciated body. He tried to appear groomed, but in reality, he knew that he looked needy.

Over and over, he wrestled with the question, *What self-respecting ad agency would want to hire a broken and disheveled former executive?* He could see it in the eyes of the Human Resources personnel of the many companies he visited. He knew what they were thinking; *"He caused the demise of his own company. What damage could he do to someone else's?"*

The fifteen-block walk back to his apartment was sobering, just like all those before. He unlocked the door of his fourth-floor flat and walked into a room of gray painted walls, poster artwork, and skimpy surroundings. Definitely not the possessions of someone to be envied any longer.

He sat in the straight-legged chair with the padded seat and solid wood backing. It probably had been part of a dining set in its better days, but now it was part of the living room decor. He decided to turn on the old 19-inch color TV. As he flipped through the channels, he stumbled briefly upon "It's a Wonderful Life" and half-a-dozen other shows with Santa Claus joyfully presented. A thought began to form in his head. *It's seasonal work, but didn't one of the nearby stores advertise for more Santas? I could do that,* he mused. *Tomorrow. Let's see them turn down a black Santa. See if the ACLU works at Christmas!*

The next morning, Brad dressed a little more casually. It didn't make his shrinking frame look quite so wiry. He pushed through the doors of Baker's Department Store and followed the signs to Human Resources. Although the store had been open only fifteen minutes, seven hopeful Santa candidates were already ahead of him. Some looked needy, just like him, but others looked more like the stereotypical elf with a rotund belly and cheerful cheeks.

He greeted the young assistant at the desk and was given paperwork to complete. Finding his way to one of the padded office chairs, he began the painful reminiscing of his past work life. Twenty minutes later, he handed over his paperwork and waited until his name was called.

Finally, a door to one of the offices opened and he was asked to enter. "I'm Ms. Pennington," greeted the tall sinewy blond woman. Her glasses and smart dress exemplified business.

"Please have a seat while I read over your application."

She frowned as she appeared to be forming questions in her mind. When she finally finished, she smiled pleasantly and began, "You have a very impressive résumé, Mr. Adams. I'm surprised that you are still unemployed; however, I'm sure that it's hard to start over. In any case, I'll come right out and say it. You surprise me. Why do you want this job?"

Brad thought a moment and decided to be painfully honest. "I need it." But he also remembered his adman background and the need to sell, even himself.

"I'm also very good at reading people, and I know what they want and what I can make them want. I've spent years giving people that. It doesn't matter what age…children, adults, seniors. I can make anyone happy, and I can help them to see that they want whatever item you want to push. Who better than Santa Claus to do that?"

He seems enthusiastic enough, thought Ms. Pennington. *A Santa trained in advertising just might work, and it doesn't hurt to have more people of color employed in that role. Heaven knows our customers reflect color!*

"OK, Mr. Adams, be here at 9:30 a.m. tomorrow. Bring your social security card and proof of citizenship. I'll check references today. You can pick up your costume on the lower level. See Mr. Santee in the service department. He'll give you the training schedule. You'll get employment papers and information tomorrow, too." As an afterthought, she interjected, "Oh, and don't ever wear the costume to the store. Just try it on first thing and let us know if any alterations need to be made. Other than padding," she added after glancing at his slender frame.

"Thank you, Ms. Pennington. I'll be here." With that he rose and shook her hand, and exited as fast as he could. The walk home was shorter and a little lighter, but still he couldn't fight the notion that he had fallen so far.

He ate his usual can of something or other and went to bed being sure to set his alarm in time for tomorrow's first day of employment. The first in nine months, he reminded himself.

The orientation went fine the next morning. With enough padding and a hefty fake beard, he actually could see himself as a jolly, roly-poly Santa Claus. By two that afternoon, he was out on the floor giving relief to the beleaguered Santa before him.

His first customer was a boy of about three. Brad could tell that the child wasn't terribly sure if this Santa was "OK." It took a little coaxing and a few cheerful chuckles along with his mom's gentle urging before the boy agreed to sit on Santa's lap.

"Now what do you want for Christmas, young man?" Brad asked.

The little boy looked up into Brad's eyes and decided it was OK to spill his heart's desire.

"I want a Tickle Me Elmo."

"Have you been a good boy?"

"Yessss," he answered and you could see the wheels turning. A good boy should get more than one thing!

"And I want a log cabin playhouse and drums, and candy and…"

As Brad listened to child after child, he realized once again what a good job the advertisers did on TV. If he really wanted to help the store and prove his worth, he should find out what they have and maybe direct any child uncertain of his or her heart's desire in that direction. He could do it, and parents wouldn't have a clue that TV wasn't the only way to market. He vowed to walk through the store's toy department when he got off at six that night.

As he clocked out and removed his suit, he carefully folded it and placed it in his assigned locker. From there he headed to the toy department. He smiled as he watched children race to specific items and plead with their parents to get that for them for Christmas. *I used to make that happen,* he thought.

Over the next few days, he did exactly as he anticipated. He tried to match any undecided child with a toy that he thought would be appropriate and would help to move store merchandise. *Just like Miracle on 34th Street,* he chuckled to himself. He soon realized that it wasn't just the idea of helping the store and getting noticed, but he thoroughly enjoyed the children and helping to determine what would brighten their little souls on Christmas morning.

As he expected, it wasn't long before his initiative was noticed. Mr. Brown, Brad's supervisor, asked to speak with him before the start of his Santa shift.

"Brad, you do a wonderful job with the children, and you've helped us to move much more merchandise than we expected. I took the liberty of reviewing your application and I see that you are really overqualified for this job."

At that, Brad, felt humbled. At one time, the compliment would have meant nothing to him. He didn't need to feel validated by anyone but himself back then.

Mr. Brown continued, "I'd like for you to stop by Human Resources. I think that we can make an offer to you that will brighten your season a bit more."

"Thank you, sir," was all that Brad managed to say.

When he arrived at the Human Resources office, Ms. Pennington was waiting for him.

"Come in, Mr. Adams. We've noticed that you managed to bring your extensive background into your current position. We've been looking for an assistant buyer in the toy department and we think your background could help us. You seem to know what people want. We think you may be the best answer to what we hope to accomplish. You would help purchase for fourteen stores initially and then maybe branch out to some of our other areas. Are you interested?"

When the reality of the offer finally sunk in, Brad was elated. "Of course, I'm interested. When would I begin?"

"Well," she answered, "We'd also like you to train our other Santas, and then later the other sales associates to do what you've been doing. You can start that training tomorrow."

She passed information across the desk that gave salary and compensation information. It wasn't anywhere near what he had made as the owner of his own ad agency, but it was certainly within what he now considered livable limits.

"Just one thing," he mentioned. "I'll start the training tomorrow, but I would love to still be Santa at least for a couple of hours each day."

He could see the apprehension in the face of Ms. Pennington so he quickly interjected, "Of course, I could do that on my own without any further compensation."

"If you think that you could handle a 10-hour day, I guess that we would have no objection," she replied.

How could he tell her that this Santa position had been not only bread and butter to him, but had given his life meaning again? What an incredible gift he had been given! To use his knowledge and expertise, and to bring joy to the littlest of God's creatures. And then suddenly, it occurred to him that this was an answer to part of his prayer from nearly two weeks ago. His soul rejoiced, but just as quickly, he remembered the other part of his prayer. His family. *At least I can now send something nice to them,* he thought.

Later that evening, he called his sister-in-law to ensure that whatever he sent to his family would still be received there. He hadn't spoken but maybe twice to Teresa since their separation. One reason was due to cost of the phone call, but most importantly, he couldn't bear to hear her voice and know what he had lost.

Three rings later the phone was answered by his wife. "Brad?" she asked.

He was surprised that she would know that it was he on the end of the other line, but maybe the generic number of the calling card gave it away.

"Teresa, I'm so sorry. How are the kids? How are you?"

Unexpectedly the reply came hurriedly. "I miss you, Brad. The kids miss you, too. We want to spend Christmas with you. Can we come?"

After fighting back tears, he quietly answered, "You can't imagine how much I want that."

When details had been worked out, he sat back in the old stick chair and closed his eyes. "Thank you, God," was all that he managed to say. Suddenly, he saw before him an angel. She was tall with wavy brown hair and green eyes. Her gown was adorned with lace and pearls on the bodice and the silken fabric of the full to-the-floor length skirt hung in cascades. A light encircled her head and he could just barely see billowy wings from behind her. She was beautiful and unearthly. "I'm Meredith, but you can call me Merry. I'm your Christmas angel, and God says, 'You're welcome'."

It was moments before Brad could stop staring. Finally, he asked, "You heard my prayer?"

"No, but God did. Life has meaning only when you serve your fellow beings. And today, you realized that your gifts could reflect good for other people. There will still be bumps in the road along life's journey, but know that God listens. Just think about how many earthly angels He used to answer your prayer. Have a Merry Christmas, Brad." With that she was gone.

In the next few seconds, Brad opened his eyes and shook the haziness from his head. *Did I just dream this? Did I talk with an angel or was this some kind of vision?* he wondered. *Whatever it was, it certainly felt real,* he concluded. And that was all that mattered. His prayer had indeed been answered, and he was sure that God knew he was grateful.

Christmas came to Brad that year, just as he had prayed that it would. He greeted it with a renewed heart, focused upon what gives life true meaning; not a life others would envy, but a life lived with a grateful and generous heart.

MIKE

His M.S. hadn't progressed in the last several years, but how could it? He was on a respirator, a feeding tube, and a catheter, and the only normal thing he could do was to have a bowel movement. Fortunately, the adult diapers kept that from being worse than it could have been. But all in all, lying virtually paralyzed day after day had not caused him to lose his will to live. In fact, he would take deep breaths to answer "yes" when asked if he felt that he had a quality of life. Go figure.

Mike was an inspiration to everyone who met him. Whether it was the hospital staff who attended to him during his many stays for urinary, respiratory, or wound infections, or his incredible ability to bounce back in the face of life-threatening occurrences, he amazed people. He was ready to meet God directly when the time came, but for now he was content being on this earth and around his mother, sister, and other family.

He had been diagnosed at twenty-four years of age and his M.S. soon became rapidly progressive. The disease took hold and each attack took a further toll on his body. Within five years he was in a wheelchair. Within ten, he was non-ambulatory, and at forty-one he was still here, barely. His mother quit her promising career in the corporate world to care for him when it became apparent that a nursing home could not provide the care necessary to keep him from experiencing frequent hospital emergencies. Bette never complained and took it as her personal responsibility to see her son through this trial. Later, his sister and her children, along with those provided by the Visiting Nurses group, would help. But, it was still Bette who felt his every pain and remained by her son's side year after year.

As Christmas approached, Mike was a little more restless than usual. He was missing something, and that something was his daughter. He did get to see her every summer for a couple of weeks, but it was hard. She was a teenager now and she couldn't expect to be seated constantly at the side of someone who couldn't interact with her, even if that was her father.

Mike hadn't spent Christmas with Molly since she was a baby. That was before her mother decided that Mike's future wasn't a promising one and she should leave before things got much worse. That was also years ago, Mike reflected. Still he would love one more Christmas with Molly. See her open the gift that he always sent annually. See her smile. See her enjoy the season. See her spend it with family, his family. He wanted to give her everything, but it was simply not possible in the current situation. Still, Mike prayed. "Dear God, Let me have Christmas with my daughter. I want to spend it with my family. I want laughter and excitement and joy. I want to know that pleasure on this earth. And we both know that there can't be many more of those earth days left," he added before again falling asleep.

His next recollection was Bette gently nudging him to awake. "Honey, it's time for your medication. Sara's here." Sara was the visiting nurse who made periodic checks on her homebound patients.

"So, how are we doing today, Mike?" she asked.
Mike took in a deep breath and made an audible "OK."

"Your mom said you were smiling when she woke you up. Was that for me?" Sara laughed.

At that point, Mike mouthed, "I had a great idea." He then tried a smile of his own.

Sara and Bette worked over and around Mike making sure he was properly positioned, clean, all tubes working as they should, meds given, and that he was as comfortable as possible. Bette couldn't help but wonder what "great idea" Mike had conjured up. He was a dreamer, she mused. He could basically do nothing for himself, yet he always had dreams. Silently she often prayed that his dreams would someday be met in Heaven. She knew with almost certainty that it wasn't going to happen here on earth.

As the holidays approached, Mike was content to hear the sounds of the season. Whether it was his mother playing

Christmas carols for him, or just the hustle and bustle of preparing for the day, it was comforting. They discussed what to send Molly again this year as well as other gifts he wished to give, but Mike couldn't forget his prayer. Silently, he felt strongly that it would be answered. He didn't know how, especially since it was an expensive ticket to fly Molly from Florida to Topeka. And at the holidays, prices were even higher. Still, he felt that God would grant him the answer to his prayer.

He chose not to share his "secret" with anyone. Although he was almost 100 percent certain that it would come true, he didn't want to spoil the surprise. He also had to admit that he didn't want to disappoint anyone in the unlikelihood that his prayer wasn't answered. But that wasn't going to happen. He knew it and that positive thought continued almost to Christmas.

As Christmas eve approached, Mike had to admit that his glowing certainty that Molly would spend Christmas with him was getting dimmer by the minute. Still, he had trouble believing that God wouldn't answer his prayer. He was sure that the very confidence he felt came from God Himself. As Mike closed his eyes that night, he drifted to sleep and awakened to a jubilant Christmas morning.

"Mike, guess who's here to spend Christmas with us?" his mother stated excitedly. "It's Molly!"

Mike couldn't believe his eyes. Yes, she was here! And she brought the present that he had sent to her so that he could see her open it. And she brought presents for everyone as well. His eyes filled with tears, and as Molly took his hand, he tried to expel enough breath to say, "I love you."

"I love you, too, Dad. And I'm so glad to be here with you and Grandma Bette, and everyone!"

She talked on and on. Just as teenagers do when talking to each other. Mike watched her animated expressions as she told him about every little thing. From the cute boy whose locker was just down from hers at the high school to the peanuts they served on the plane. And, when all the presents had been opened, dinner had been served, and the spirit of love was bountiful around them, Mike actually woke up.

At first, he couldn't believe that he had been dreaming. He soon realized that he had only dreamt that he awakened earlier. Molly wasn't here. And finally, that his prayer wasn't answered. For the first time in a very long while, Mike felt downhearted. He was so sure God was going to answer this prayer. Would he really have to wait for Heaven to actually celebrate a Christmas with his daughter?

Just then, Bette came into the room. "Hi, Honey," she cheerfully and quietly spoke. "Merry Christmas. It's almost ten and I've got a little surprise for you."

At that, Mike perked up a little, and it took him briefly away from his overwhelming disappointment. "I've got Molly on the line for you and she sent a picture of herself on e-mail so we could see her opening your present."

"Hi, Dad. I love you," she began. Bette placed her on speaker phone and then she talked on and on. It wasn't the way Mike thought that his prayer would be answered, but he had to admit, that it was answered. He did get to spend Christmas with his daughter. Although it was only a forty-five-minute conversation, the joy of the season was shared. With the e-mail, he saw Molly's smile and her delight when she opened her gift. All courtesy of Bette, who arranged the phone call and unknowingly became Mike's Christmas angel—the one whom God had chosen to work through to answer his prayer.

MARSHA

It had been two years, and while she no longer cried every day, Marsha still had her moments.

"Are you crying again, Babe?" her husband asked.

Ray knew the reason, it was always the same. She missed her mother. Today, she was remembering again.

As the oldest of four sisters, it just seemed to fall to her to be her mother's main caregiver when June's failing health became an issue. Her father had died many years before and she watched as her aging mother's neurological issues worsened. Marsha also knew that her mother had a strong will and that her life had not been easy since losing the true other half of her soul when Lew died.

For years, Marsha made it a point to check on June daily, if only for a quick in-and-out visit. She also arranged and transported June and her mother-in-law to her home for weekly dinners. It was so much fun for everyone to get out of their houses, enjoy one another's company, and to receive the fun little "favors" Marsha had found each week. Unfortunately, it also fell to Marsha to attend most of the doctor appointments since the closest sister had little time between having a young family and a job that required a two-hour commute.

Sometimes June seemed depressed and reluctant to do things. Some of these things were as simple as calling the doctor or pharmacy. While her sister, who lived in the same city, added a little support, it still fell mostly to Marsha to motivate, but doing so could be very difficult. June was stubborn, and sometimes it required a direct ploy to that characteristic. Marsha found herself saying things that she knew would maybe hurt her mother, but words she also hoped would spark the stubbornness with anger and result in a positive action.

Every time her mother had to go into the hospital, Marsha was there, with the exception of one time. She and Ray had gone on vacation and were visiting another sister in California. Vicki, the sister at home, called to say that Mom had fallen again. Mom, herself, had also called the paramedics a number of times the previous night for various issues. The paramedics thought that Mom should be checked out. All seemed routine so there was no rush necessary to get back home.

When Marsha finally returned from her trip a week later, June was doing OK, but had to be moved to a longer-term facility to recuperate. She could not go directly back home to live alone, as her choice had always been. It fell to Vicki and another sister, who lived not too far away, to scout possible facilities, all the while assuring Mom that it was just temporary until she could gain strength with therapy and again live alone. The therapy worked and June did indeed go home. This at least showed Marsha that the burden could be shared, and while she would always be the main caregiver, her sisters could be trusted to help in a pinch as well. Still, it was hard to turn loose from the obligation that Marsha felt.

June had bounced back on so many occasions. She had endured a broken leg twice, two prostheses in her hip, a crack in her sacrum, a heart attack, another heart issue, severe urinary tract infections requiring hospitalization, and respiratory distress. Every time her daughters, and some doctors, thought that this was "it," June surprised and delighted everyone with a more or less speedy recovery. She was even sent home with Hospice once, and within a week, no longer required them.

It was months later when June had another serious issue and this is what Marsha was remembering today. And so this last and final event, Marsha recalled, appeared to be just another in a long history. June was eighty-seven and frail, but she still had the same "makeup" as "stubborn ol' June."

This was again a serious respiratory complication. She spent some time in the hospital, but again required convalescence at a longer-term facility. When she was moved there from the hospital, a number of issues arose. June couldn't get comfortable, the staff waited too long to take her to the bathroom, etc. The staff stated in a wee-hours-of-the-morning phone call to Marsha that June "is driving us crazy." Marsha figured out a few simple things to make it easier, and everything relaxed. While there, June received a diuretic, but was placed in an adult "pull-up" (a concession to an overworked staff that couldn't be immediately available when June needed to "go.") It was discovered later that no one had been checking to see if she was actually "going." This inattentiveness resulted in a urinary infection that attacked her entire body. She was rushed to the local hospital.

Soon after arriving, it was apparent that things weren't good. But June had surprised them so many times before. Marsha consoled herself with *Just keep pushing the antibiotics and Mom will respond.*

Marsha set up a vigil at the hospital, waiting on her mother hand and foot, and supporting the hospital staff that could not be there at a beckon call. This continued in the Intensive Care Unit when it appeared that June's urine flow was at a crucial level. Everyone knew that this was extremely serious, and Mom might not recover this time. Family graced the ICU room from wall to wall while June carried on conversations and asked to be occasionally suctioned. Her breathing was supplemented with higher amounts of oxygen, but she enjoyed the activity surrounding her bed. The ICU nurses permitted the visitations, realizing even more than the family, that this could be the final night, and requesting only that other patients not be disturbed.

Marsha had planned to spend the night and had asked a nurse friend, Saundra, to join her. When all the good-byes had been said with plans for tomorrow's visits, June continued to talk into the early morning hours to Marsha's friend. Marsha, exhausted, had fallen asleep.

Just before six that morning, Saundra awakened Marsha. "Your mom's not doing well, Marsha. They've called a code blue." Watching in horrified fashion, Marsha finally called a halt to the resuscitate order that she had made. "Stop!" was all she could manage to say, and then the tears flowed. She held her mother's hand noting the change in warmth to coldness.

"How could I have let this happen?" she cried. Guilt was consuming her and would for the next two years. "I should have known to check that Mom was urinating. I knew the symptoms. Why didn't I move her from that facility? Why, Why, Why?" she repeated over and over to her immediate family, her sisters, her friends, and anyone else who would listen.

It didn't matter that no one else saw Marsha's culpability in the matter. Marsha did and that was all that mattered to her. Rationally, she knew that you make the best decisions that you can with the available facts, but her heart said that she should have known. She also felt regret over the many fights she had "provoked" with her mother in trying to motivate her. It was all too much and she soon began "searching."

"How do you know there's really a God?" she would ask. "I wish that I could believe that there is life after death and that Mom is really with Dad now." Neither books nor others possessing a strong faith could give her the comfort that she needed. What she really needed was Mom to tell her that all was well.

As Christmas approached soon after the second anniversary of June's passing, Marsha again felt melancholy. June so enjoyed Christmas and every time Marsha put the electronic carousel on the tree, she cried. She remembered with bittersweetness, *Mom wanted that carousel so much, but didn't want to pay the price for it. Ray bought it for her and she almost squealed with delight.* She could remember some of the happy times, but still, so many memories were riddled with regret.

Now at a point of impending despair, Marsha sent up a little prayer. She had been doing that more recently. She didn't know how much it would help, but *it sure couldn't hurt.* "Oh, God, I just want peace. I want to know that Mom understands why I said and did the things I did. I want to know that she's found peace. And I want to know that she knows how much I loved her." That last thought always brought tears to her eyes, but it was her fervent hope that June knew how much Marsha loved her. After all, Marsha was always there and refused to leave her mother's side if she thought that her mother needed her. *But, did Mom really know?*

As the day of Christ's birth drew near, Marsha again tried to busy herself with diversions that would make her forget her loss, for at least a little while. She bought presents for family and had a particularly good time shopping for her four grandchildren. She planned shopping excursions, a holiday open house, and attendance at her sister's annual Christmas Eve family and friends get-together. In the back of her mind, she remembered her prayer, but still thought nothing more of it than voicing her hopes to anyone.

And then it was Christmas Eve. The last thing her sister said to her was a reminder, "Be open to contact when you sleep. Let yourself believe." Since her sister believed that she had had contact in this manner from her deceased husband, Marsha mumbled faintly, "OK. Merry Christmas."

When she and Ray had returned home from her sister's Christmas Eve open house, and made all the necessary preparations for the following day, they fell into bed ready for sleep. As lights were turned out, Marsha again decided to "voice" her soul's desire, "Mom, let me know that you are OK. Let me know that you knew how much I loved you." As an afterthought and for good measure, she added, "God, please let this happen." And then she fell asleep.

About three in the morning, Marsha's nondescript dream was interrupted. June suddenly appeared and it took Marsha only a moment to notice how wonderful her mother looked. No more being frail. No more illness. Just glowing! And she seemed more youthful and full of energy. This was the mom who could do anything. The mom of her childhood.

"Mom?" she asked in disbelief.

"Yes, Honey, it's me."

"You, you look great!" she stammered.

"I'm here because you wanted me, Marsha. God heard your prayer and He said that I could come."

"Oh, Mom," Marsha felt herself crying and shaking.

"On earth, I didn't always know why you said the things you did, but I knew you loved me. You were always there when I needed you. And I now know how much you really did for me and how hard it was for you. I do know how much you loved me and still do. And I love you, too."

Marsha was so overwhelmed that words did not come. She just stared and basked in the warmth of her mother's love.

"I have to go now, Honey. Don't worry about me. I am fine, and I am with your Dad. He loves you, too."

Marsha could see her bend over and felt her mother place a kiss on her cheek. And then she faded. Marsha immediately awoke and the place where the kiss had been planted had a faint wetness. The room was also filled with her mother's favorite perfume, Shalimar.

She placed her hand over the kiss and realized that this was more than a dream. This was contact. Her mother had many times been an angel to her, doing things for her, making her confidence stronger, and just loving her when she didn't feel very lovable. June was her Christmas angel. And, as Marsha soon realized, her prayer had been answered.

RYAN

Ryan was a marvel in many ways. From the time he was a preschooler, he could be the most stubborn child imaginable, yet also the sweetest and most sensitive. It took many years before he believed his parents that he was gifted in so many ways. He was smart, tall, handsome, and athletic. It seemed that anything that he put his mind to, he could do. His father always said, "If we could just channel the stubbornness into something positive, he would always persevere to the good." And so it was.

At age ten, Ryan came running into the house excitedly exclaiming, "I've decided that I want to pitch."

"Wonderful!" his parents both agreed. This was however a little strange since Ryan was an excellent baseball player in hitting and catching the ball. Never before had he expressed interest in pitching. His tall stature gave him a long reach when fielding balls from first or third base, and his only issue seemed to be running. He was still trying to grow into what would eventually be his 6'6" frame.

For the next five days, Ryan eagerly practiced with anyone who could be coerced into a round of "catch." His mother was initially happy to help until she realized that his throw was fast and hard enough to produce bruises on her fingers, even with a fielder's mitt.

"I think I'm ready," Ryan announced as the family was getting into the car to go to the game. "Coach said that I could pitch today!" Ryan's enthusiasm was overflowing and his confidence was just what they knew it would be. Here again, his stubbornness had simply made him practice until he knew he was good.

"That's great, Honey," said his mom. "We'll be watching, and good luck!"

About the third inning, the coach signaled for Ryan to warm up. Soon after, he replaced the tired pitcher with the rookie.

"Strike one!" yelled the umpire.

His parents looked at one another and smiled broadly. *Ryan was going to do great with this,* they thought. *Even starting later than most players in wanting to pitch, he would succeed.*

"Strike two!" came the next call.

"Ball one! Ball two!" By now, Ryan had learned to calm himself a little by trying to shake off the bad pitches, literally. It had become his endearing little quirk to shake his hand after a bad throw, willing all the bad neural directives to get lost.

Then, "Ball three!" And finally, "Strike three!"

The crowd roared, certain that the new rookie pitcher was going to do a pretty good job for the team.

Next batter, "Strike one!" Ryan was in the zone. "Strike two!" *That's it, we're getting closer!* "Ball one!" Oops, better shake that one off. "Strike three!"

OK, two down and one to go, thought Ryan.

And then it happened. A few strikes on the next three batters, but they got walks. Ryan's confidence was clearly suspect, no matter how many shakes of his hand. His self-assurance was definitely waning.

"Hey, Ryan," his coach yelled while walking to the mound. After getting Ryan's attention and then reaching him, the coach continued, "You're doing OK, but you look pretty nervous. Do you want to continue or do you want to rest?"

Clearly disappointed in his performance, Ryan chose to sit out the rest of the pitching rotation. His batting was still good so he was sure he could continue to please himself as well as the onlookers by shifting to batter and field positions.

Even though he had batted and fielded nicely, the ride home was somewhat quiet. "I didn't do well," he lamented.

"Honey, you did great," his mom tried to convince him.

"This was your first time, son," his dad told him. "You have to give it time before you can be perfect. You did fine. Just keep practicing," his dad encouraged.

"I don't know if I want to pitch anymore," came Ryan's sad response.

Over the next two days, his parents tried to be supportive saying that whatever he decided to do would be fine. And they also encouraged him to keep trying. Quitting anything that he wanted to do was very uncharacteristic of Ryan.

After the next day, Ryan was again out in the yard throwing baseballs and playing catch with anyone who would do so. He practiced grounders so that his fielding would still be tip-top and throwing different speeds and curves that his coach had taught him.

By the next game, Ryan was again ready to show that practice makes perfect, or at least acceptable in his eyes.

The second time the pitching was much improved. Ryan lasted three innings. Then five, and then he became the starting pitcher.

Ryan's strong bat and good arm made him fun to watch. In the younger leagues, pitchers could still be a part of the batting rotation. His parents delighted in attending his games. It was fun to watch him strike out batters and also hit the ball out of the park for home runs. And even though every summer vacation had to be taken after the first part of August in order to not conflict with the baseball schedule, it was something the entire family was willing to do. Even his slightly older brother agreed.

This live-for-summer-baseball mentality continued all through his years in school, eventually resulting in a pitching spot on the high school varsity team his senior year. In fact, it was really quite odd when Ryan finally stopped playing baseball in the summer; his parents weren't quite sure what to do with the time!

During his senior year in high school, Ryan gave some thought to playing college ball. He loved the game, but wasn't sure that he wanted to devote the required time to practice. College meant studying, and more importantly, college social life. Those would require more of his attention, not baseball.

Off and on after high school graduation, Ryan played recreational baseball in the summer, but most often city league basketball. That, too, was a sport he loved and had played on his junior high team. Ryan was athletic and simply good at sports, much to his father's pride.

Unfortunately, Ryan's freshman year in college wasn't the most promising. Too much partying, late-night socializing, and not enough studying caused some academic performance issues. This would follow him through another year and a half of college. Finally, when he decided to become a serious student, he was twenty-five and working part-time. It now meant that he had to retake some classes as replacement hours to increase his GPA.

During his first years in college, Ryan was having difficulty deciding on what he really wanted to do. That was not unexpected as he had shown interest in many things while growing up. When he was five years old, he wanted to be an ice-cream truck driver until he discovered that drivers still had to pay for the ice cream they ate. Soon after, he discovered the love of reading. All through grade school and junior high, being an author was his goal. It was a very plausible one because his writing was exceptional.

By high school, Ryan had discovered the excitement of computers through an advanced class. Although he had many talents and abilities, programming seemed to be where his interests lay. Or, at least until his senior year in high school when he decided that programming was not "social" enough. He wanted to do something with more interpersonal interaction.

So, it wasn't too much of a surprise that Ryan had trouble committing to a career goal. Besides wanting the fun of college life, he really had no idea of what he wanted to do as a career.

During high school and college, he became good friends with the youth leader at his church, Dave, who introduced him to many provocative religious works. Ryan later found himself as a confirmation leader with the youth. He accompanied the youth group on summer work conferences and helped lead them through their own faith journeys. It was no surprise when later, after dropping out of college, Ryan announced to his parents, "I want to be a high school teacher." His parents always thought that he might go into youth ministry, but he quickly shared that he felt that he "couldn't go anywhere else with that." God called him for something else.

While Ryan was waiting to re-enter college to pursue his now firm goal, his father lost his battle with cancer. The drive and will simply left Ryan for a little more than a year, but with gentle nudging from his mother, he again began taking classes.

After another three years and at age twenty-eight, Ryan announced, "Mom, I've got my degree and I have a job offer at St. Martin's, teaching philosophy and psychology to juniors and seniors."

With typical pride in her son's accomplishments, she replied, "Ryan, I'm so proud of you! The girls will love you because you are so handsome, and the boys will respect you because of your large stature. It's perfect!" With that she pulled his face lower and gave him a peck on the cheek. "And your dad would be so proud, too, son."

The next few years were interesting. Ryan discovered a new love by way of one of his teaching colleagues. Like him, she was in her twenties. And, strangely enough, the students were actually eager to learn. He enjoyed the lively discussions that they had regarding philosophical issues and exploring psychological implications of various actions. *What a great life,* he thought. But, there was always something missing when he went to St. Martin's baseball games. It was certainly fun, especially with Beth by his side, but the "what if" scenario was always plaguing him. He wondered how many of those students who played baseball would someday pursue what he chose not to, and how many others would have little pangs of regret and their own "what ifs."

In October, Ryan was watching yet another World Series on TV.

"Ryan, are you going to watch that all afternoon?" Beth asked from the kitchen. "It seems we just go from baseball, to football, to basketball. Thank heavens you aren't a lover of soccer and hockey, too!" she sighed.

"I just want to see a little more of this, Hon," he replied. "Then I'll come help you. I know our mothers are coming over for dinner so just tell me what you want me to do and I'll do it." *But not too soon*, he hoped. *I really want to see this game.*

As he watched, Ryan was suddenly moved to send up his usual little half prayer, half thought. He had been growing a little anxious lately and the "what if" was slowly creeping back into his consciousness now and then. "I'd really like to be involved in sports again, God," he began. "It's harder for me to find the time to play now, but I just want to be back into it somehow. I don't know how to do that and not take a lot of time away from my family." And then he was interrupted again by Beth.

"Ryan, can you get the big salad bowl down for me? It's on the highest shelf and I can't reach it. Sorry, Honey, but I need it now." Beth felt a little guilty about calling him away from the Series. He watched a lot of sports, and she knew how much he really loved them. Silently she was glad he hadn't pursued a career as a "jock," but she knew that sometimes he felt a little cheated by not having done so.

After Thanksgiving, they had both settled into finalizing the semester. Last-minute pushes to finish the texts and then finals. Everything had to be done before Christmas break which left only three weeks. It was good that most sports were finished until the new year. At least that meant fewer outside distractions, mused Beth.

And then, a week before Christmas, the Principal, Dan James, called Ryan into his office.

"Ryan, I have a proposal for you," he began. "Al Woods and his wife are having a baby soon and he has asked to take family medical leave. This is his second marriage and I guess he doesn't want this baby to grow up not knowing who he is. That means he doesn't want to coach anymore after he returns in three months. I know you have an interest in sports. You played them in school, and you helped coach some, too. With the city league and some youth groups?"

"Yes," confirmed Ryan, wondering where this conversation was leading.

"Think you could take over the baseball team this spring?" asked Dan.

"Of course!" Ryan replied without a moment's hesitation. "I'd love to do that!" Then remembering how much he enjoyed teaching his advanced classes, he asked, "Would I still teach my same courses, too?"

"I don't think that would be a problem, unless you do," the principal responded. "Of course, there would be an increase in pay, too, to compensate for the extra time spent coaching."

After the details had been worked out for Ryan to assume coaching duties, he quickly thought with whom he wanted to share this great news...*Beth, Mom, my brother*...And as he was walking away thinking of how perfect this opportunity would be, he suddenly stopped. *My prayer! I'm going to be involved in sports again! It isn't playing, but Hallelujah!*

Christmas time brought the offer to Ryan. But God found a way to turn one person's decision, that of the coach, into an answer to Ryan's prayer made in October. The lucky message bearer and Christmas angel, in this instance, was the principal. But those most benefited would be the baseball team members who found their own angel in the wisdom, encouragement, and skills of Ryan.

JILL

Jill had only one real wish this Christmas and that was to spend it with her seven-year-old son, Joshua. She knew that really wasn't a possibility since she had shared custody with her ex-husband and this was his year. Mark never varied their schedule no matter what. But still she wanted to see Josh's eyes light up when he received the Nintendo Wii she had scrimped and saved for during the last six months. And truth be told, the breast cancer scare had made her focus even more on what was really important to her. As if it weren't already her son, she mused.

Suddenly she was awakened out of her daydream to a ringing phone. Jill picked up the phone and heard her son's excited voice, "Hi, Mom, it's me. David Gibbons got sick so I got his part in the school play. I'm a wise man!"

Well, that could be appropriate at times or at least some derivative of that anyway! Jill thought. After all, he was seven and sometimes tried to assert his independence a little less appropriately than he should. Later she would explain to him that the role was actually "wiseman" and not pronounced as two separate words.

"That's great, Honey," she managed to say. "When is it?"

"Next Friday night at seven. We have to be there early 'cause I have to get dressed and all of that."

"OK, Hon, we'll make it happen. I'll see you at three, after school."

That really was wonderful, Jill thought as she remembered how Josh had struggled through school these past two years after the divorce. To actually be excited by something at school really was a blessing. Then just as quickly, she thought *UGH. I'll have to tell Mark about this, too, and he doesn't like short notices with his busy work schedule. He's got a little under two weeks to schedule. Well, too bad. His son should come first. And he was the one who chose to pay for this private parochial school!*

Jill and Mark had married soon after college, and their life together looked very promising. She had received her degree in child development and he in business administration. After working a few years in their chosen fields, Mark decided to pursue an MBA. Although it again put a hamper into their finances, they rationalized that it would be well worth the cost. They would just have to delay having a family a little longer. Or so was the plan. Three months after Mark started the program, Jill became pregnant with Josh. Since he had only been working part-time and then devoting full time to his studies, this meant a major change. Now the time for work and studies would have to be reversed. Mark would have to work full-time and then pursue the MBA part-time. While both wanted the baby, Mark secretly resented having to postpone his dream. It was, after all, his dream for all of them.

It didn't take long to realize where Mark's interest really lay. He loved his son, but his career was just too important. His success wasn't just for his family anymore; it was for the pursuit of all things possessive. Jill was dependable and thoughtful, but a trophy wife she wasn't. She had more interest in her son than her husband's career and that wasn't Mark's idea of an ideal marriage. He wanted someone who would appreciate him and his accomplishments more. When Josh was five, they divorced, but agreed to share custody. To make things easier on Josh and his schooling, as well as Mark's busy career, they settled on alternate holidays. Summers with Mark, and the school year with Jill. This was especially workable for everyone since Mark now lived an hour away.

Jill began planning the next two hours. *Let's see. In the meantime, I can go pick up his Nintendo Wii and wrap it. That will be a nice surprise under the tree for him.* Josh had certainly been counting every present. Now that he no longer believed in Santa Claus, he knew that all good things would come from Mom and Dad. And while Dad could spend a little more guilt money on buying him things, he knew that he could always count on Mom to come up with something good, too. He would receive his Dad's presents at Mark's house this year, so the only presents he could count right now would be the ones Jill gave him.

Jill dropped by the bank to withdraw her Christmas Club money. She had enough to buy the Nintendo Wii and some leftover money for a nice gift for her parents. She would spend Christmas with them as she had every year since the divorce. They lived five hours away and she always flew because "you could never tell what the weather is going to do." Or, at least, that is what her mother always said. *Mom isn't paying for this ticket either,* Jill thought, but she knew that her mother was right. St. Louis winters could be pretty strange, not to mention those near Kansas City where Jill lived. And driving could be more "iffy" than flying.

From the bank, she went to the store where she had placed the game system on hold. They had her credit card number, but she preferred to pay cash. It was too easy to let credit cards get out of hand as she had already learned. She didn't need any more interest added to what she was already paying on her Visa. Buying the Wii was a financial stretch, but knowing how much Josh would love it made it worth the sacrifice.

She arrived back home at 2:30 p.m., with just enough time to wrap the gift and then get Josh from school. *Oh drat,* she remembered, *I have to call Mark about the play. Maybe I'd better do that before I wrap the present. I can do that later,* she resolved reluctantly.

"Mr. Korchak, please," she told the company operator.

Soon after Mark came on the line. "What is it, Jill? I'm in the middle of putting together a presentation."

Just what I expected, thought Jill. He usually took her calls but was always annoyed that she had interrupted his important work.

"Josh got a wonderful part in a school play and it's next Friday."

"Couldn't you have called me earlier? It's busy here and that's less than two weeks away," Mark grumbled.

She struggled to control her own irritation. "I just found out, Mark, and that is why I'm calling. I thought you might want as much notice as possible so that you can be there."

'OK, thanks. I'll try," and then he hung up.

Same ol' Mark, thought Jill. *Too busy to talk to me. Too busy for his son. But he'll try!*

She tried to put the conversation out of her mind and looked at her watch. *That was a short enough conversation. Maybe I do have time to wrap the Wii real quick,* she figured. Taking it out of the sack and choosing just the right paper, she managed to make a pretty impressive and enticing present. She knew Josh was at an age when what was inside was more important, but the better it was wrapped, the better the present!

She pushed it under the tree along with his other four inexpensive gifts and rushed out the door to the car. Ten minutes later she was sitting in front of the school waiting for Josh.

Soon, he came out of the building on a dead run to the car. He was lugging his backpack that appeared to be stuffed like a sack.

"I've got my costume, Mom. They said you might have to make it fit me better. You can just paste it."

Jill thought a moment and was a little incredulous. "Are you sure they said I could use paste on it, Josh?" she asked.

"Well, paste or something else like it," he conceded.

Deciphering what Josh really meant was an on-going challenge sometimes. Thinking of all the words that sounded like paste, she came up with, "How about baste?" adding a half chuckle.

"Yeah, maybe. What's baste?" He sounded even more confused by that than "paste."

"You know, like what you helped me to do the turkey to keep it moist last Thanksgiving? But it can also mean a temporary stitch, and I can do that," she replied.

"Great, Mom." And with that, the conversation was finished. For the ride home, Josh immersed himself in looking at his costume and reviewing the sheet for his five lines that would signal his acting debut.

When they arrived home, Josh quickly noticed his new present. "Can I shake it?" he asked.

"Not unless you want to break it," his mother sternly warned.

Each day, Josh would look at the present, hold it and smile. Jill knew that he had probably guessed correctly as to its contents. She also noticed how eager her son was to go to school. They were practicing intently for the play, and she even noticed that he was more interested than usual in his studies.

Finally, the Wednesday before the play, Mark called.

"I'm going to make the play," he announced. "Since we're so close to Christmas, why don't I just pick up Josh early, after the play, and take him with me? I've arranged a sitter and he should only miss a day or two of school."

"But he'll miss his parties at school, Mark. Not to mention any assignments for over the break," Jill protested. "And I really want some time with him, too, Mark. And a sitter?" she half demanded.

"Yes, Jill, a sitter. And if you're honest, you don't like it because it's probably more of an inconvenience to you than to Josh. You get him far more than I do, and I can at least have time with him this weekend and a little in the evenings before Christmas. Sandy's daughter will be here, too, so they can play together during the day with the sitter. You can fight this all you want, but you know that I'm entitled to this one concession."

Jill's immediate response was *Ugh! Sandy, Mark's new girlfriend. Well, maybe not new since they had known each other before the divorce. And maybe more than just "know." Sandy would be a trophy wife. She had her own career and was just as absorbed in it as Mark's. Her poor daughter! When they marry, they had better have good medical insurance for a therapist for poor Amy,* she thought. *Now I have to break the news to Josh. Thanks, Mark,* she grimaced.

"But I don't want to go early, Mom," her son pleaded. "I don't want to play with Amy and I don't want a stupid ol' sitter. Please, Mom, don't make me go."

"Honey, you know that your Dad doesn't get to spend as much time with you as he would like," she half lied. *He gets all the time he really wants,* she thought angrily. But she would never share this opinion with her son. "I would love you to stay longer until Christmas, too, but it wouldn't be fair to your Dad."

At that, Josh turned to run while crying and shouting, "I don't care if it's fair to him. It's not fair to me!"

Although she felt that it wasn't the right thing to do because of her own feelings, she hurt for her son and decided to pray.

"God, please let Josh stay with me this Christmas. I need him and he needs me. I know that it isn't right for me to ask this, but if it can be your will, please make it happen."

Jill noticed that Josh's mood the next two days was heavier now. He was still interested in the play and his latest present, but he was definitely close to pouting. They packed his bag before going to the play and placed it in the trunk of the car. She also included a small gift for Mark from Josh. Her son hadn't been interested in shopping for his Dad now so Jill bought the obligatory tie. It was not too loud, but very business like. Very Mark.

She and Mark sat at opposite ends of the auditorium and at the conclusion of the play, they both applauded with exaggerated enthusiasm. Each trying to show how much they loved their son who could see them from the stage. When the curtain was drawn, Mark moved quickly to Jill.

"I need to talk with you," he said.

"There's nothing to talk about, Mark. He doesn't really want to go early. I've got his things in the car." With that she started to turn away.

"No, wait," Mark said while grabbing her arm. "That's what I want to talk with you about. Something's come up. I need to change plans so Josh will need to be with you this Christmas. Can you do it?"

At first, Jill wanted to remind Mark how unyielding he had always been with "the schedule," but just as quickly she realized what a blessing had just occurred.

"What? Oh sure," she stammered. "Do you want to tell him or should I?"

"I'll do it," he said. "I'll tell him now and we can discuss it more on the way back to my place tonight. There is a big company cruise right after Christmas and a select few from our office are invited along with some of our best clients. Rob Bernstein was going to do a presentation onboard, but he had emergency gall bladder surgery and they asked me to do it. I need to prepare for the presentation and I wouldn't really have much time to spend with Josh after this weekend so it wouldn't be fair to him. I'll take Josh now and have him back to you on Sunday afternoon. That way he can still attend his school parties and he won't have to be with a babysitter."

As he watched Jill's expression turn to one of happiness, he managed a smile of his own.

"That isn't a problem at all, Mark," Jill gushed. "Just let me congratulate him on his stellar performance. And thank you," she said while giving him a quick peck on the cheek. "Thank you for Josh <u>and</u> for me."

Her life had just been given a jolt of pure unadulterated joy! And then she realized that her prayer had been answered, and as funny as it was, Mark had been the messenger. He was her Christmas angel! The best part is that Mark had shown true consideration for Josh by deciding what would actually be best for him. And when she saw Mark talking to Josh and the smile on Josh's face, Jill knew that all she wanted for Christmas would come true.

ROBERT

Robert slouched in the crowded waiting room of the free clinic and tried to remember how he had ended up in this situation. It wasn't really too hard. He had made some stupid mistakes that had cost him dearly. He was happy once. And healthy. But that was before. Before his wife left him. Before he lost his good-paying construction job. Before his friends gave up on him as a lost cause. Before his social drinking became something more. Thankfully the rest of his family had disowned him long before the other things. At least he didn't have to worry about them.

Now he was alone…again, even in this crowded waiting room. No one wanted near the man who was hacking loudly and shaking with every breath. Yes, he was alone, just as he had been for the past three years. Street living and the occasional shelter don't give a person much chance to form relationships, he knew.

Wandering from town to town, and now settled here. The wandering days were finally over. This was his second visit to the clinic in a week. The staff had told him a month and a half ago that "things would get worse." *Yeah, right,* he thought. *I'm thirty-two and dying of lung cancer. All they can do is try to take the pain away. At least the physical pain,* he mused. *Get worse? Yeah, bring it on!*

He waited another forty-five minutes lost in thought before his name was called.

"Mr. Greene?" the nurse, who had just stepped through the medical treatment section, called.

"I'm here," he answered. With effort he lifted his diminishing frame from the chair and walked slowly over to the door that Nurse Grindell was holding open.

"Not doing so well today?" she questioned.

"Nope. I'm really hurting again. My whole chest just aches. The headaches are worse and I've got bad tremors." His only consolation was that he would soon receive more morphine patches and then be edged into a calming state of oblivion.

As they reached the examination room, Nurse Grindell sat across from him and opened the blood pressure cuff. "I need to take your vitals," she announced. As she did so, she asked, "Are you still smoking, Mr. Greene?" Her question was routine, but there was just a tinge of rebuke in it.

Robert stiffened momentarily. *She may be required to ask this question each visit, but she knew. She could smell it, so why ask? Does she really think I quit since Tuesday?*

"Yes," he replied quietly. *Of course I am, damn it,* he thought. *I'm sick. I'm dying. I can't eat so I might as well get enjoyment out of something!* All of that is what he really wanted to say. Even alcohol didn't hold temptation for him anymore. He still wanted it, but it wasn't good with the medicine and he would just throw it up anyway. He couldn't even keep it down long enough to feel any effect. The vomiting took away what little breath he had, and soon the punitive aspects of it eased him off of the bottle, but not the cigarettes. They only made him cough more and he was already doing that. Whenever he could bum one, he would. The change that he could panhandle also went for the little white sticks that caused what was killing him.

As she finished, Nurse Grindell rose from her chair and announced, "I'll let the doctor know you are here."

Again, he sat waiting, only this time he was physically alone with his thoughts. *Just give me more morphine,* he repeated over and over to himself.

Finally, Dr. Steele rapped on the door and entered. "Not doing so well today, huh, Robert?" he asked.

"*Well, duh!*" Robert wanted to say. Instead he settled on a brief "no."

"I see that you are still smoking," the doctor read aloud. Glancing at his patient, he decided not to go any further with a lecture. It had all been discussed, many times before. He would be dead soon, and although smoking was making things a little worse, trying to go cold turkey for something that wouldn't make a difference made little sense.

"Describe your pain for me," Dr. Steele said.

Just as he was about to answer, Robert went into one of his frequent hacking fits. It was painful to watch, especially for medically trained personnel who could envision what was happening with this living, but deteriorating, body before them.

When he had finished, Robert looked at the doctor with tears that had been forced with the cough's racking pain. "My chest feels like I have a ton on it. I can't get my breath and the cough shakes my whole body. My head aches really bad and my tremors are worse. I'm hurtin', Doc," he murmured.

"I see that you are, Robert," came the compassionate response. "Let me get some more patches for you. I think we need to double what you have. You're staying at the shelter?" Dr. Steele confirmed.

"Yes," answered Robert quietly. He didn't want the coughing to start again, so no voice straining.

"I'll go get them now," the doctor announced. "You know what to do. Have the shelter call me if you get worse and can't make it back here."

Dr. Steele had been saying that last part for the past two weeks. *If I didn't know I was getting worse, those comments would tell me,* Robert thought.

Soon, Nurse Grindell entered with the new patches. "You know how to do these, right?" she asked.

With a shake of his head for affirmation, Robert rose and took the patches from her hands. "Thanks. See ya' soon," he mumbled.

As he walked back to the shelter, he tried to stay warm. Walking was a feat that was becoming more and more difficult. Bad nutrition, an illness that was attacking his body, and ever-weakening muscles made the trek to the shelter progressively slower and more painful.

It was nearing Christmas and even the bright lights adorning the decorations of the storefronts and lampposts could not lessen the despair he was feeling. He lifted his head once and saw a happy mother and young child blissfully discussing what Santa might bring. They were looking forward to the holiday, one that was surely to be Robert's last.

After eight blocks, he knocked on the door to the shelter. Everyone else had to wait until five each night before they could be admitted, but Robert had special privileges. He was dying so the shelter administration made special accommodations for him. His cot was away from others and he was permitted to come and go pretty much as he wished. Food was never an issue because he really didn't want any.

He made himself eat only a little something during breakfast and dinner. It made the staff feel better, and he knew it was necessary in order for him to maintain any independence.

With regret, he thought, *soon enough, the shelter staff will call hospice and I will be sent somewhere else to die.* Unless, of course, he could just die in his sleep at the shelter. That was what he truly hoped.

After Tate opened the door for him, he looked at Robert and said, "You don't look so good, Robbie." Tate was the only one who could get by with calling him Robbie. That was his childhood nickname, but no one had called him that since eighth grade. Tate was fatherly and so Robert allowed the moniker.

"I'm feeling pretty bad, Tate," he confessed. "I've got more patches. Can you put the rest away in the medicine lockbox for me? I'm just gonna use one now," he said.

Tate's watchful gaze as Robert shuffled over to his cot was not lost on Robert. He and Tate had become friends, somewhat. Or really more like father and son strangely enough. He knew Tate cared, and all Robert really wanted was to leave this world knowing someone would give a crap. And then he remembered how kind Tate had really been to him. Giving him meds in the middle of the night, crying with him over the diagnosis (*although ending all of this had its good points, too,* he thought). Tate always saw that Robert had enough blankets and whatever he wanted to eat, whenever and however that rarely occurred.

A little smile crossed his face as he once again realized, *it's Christmas and this man is worried about me. Somebody does give a crap, after all,* he mused. *I wish that I could give him something,* he thought. And although he hadn't really prayed in some time, he quickly sent up a little request. *God, if you're there, I haven't done much for anyone in my life, and I've made a terrible mess of it. But please, God, help me to give something to Tate.* At that, he quickly put on a new patch, hoping that it would soon take away the pain, at least for awhile. When his head hit the pillow, he fell into an exhausted sleep.

It was six in the evening when he awoke. Tate had just come into the room to announce that dinner was being served. "You want anything, Robbie?"

As grogginess slowly left his head, Robert sat up and looked at Tate. "I'm not hungry...as usual," he added. "But I'll try a little something."

"OK, good," Tate answered and turned to leave.

"Hey, Tate," Robert called. "If you could have anything in the world, what would it be?"

Looking back at Robert, he wondered why such a man would ask as strange a question as that. "Why? You win the lottery or something?" he joked.

"Nah, just wondering," Robert said. The idea was to find out what Tate really wanted in this life. Maybe if he knew what Tate wanted, he could come up with something in that theme.

"Oh, a thousand bucks, new car, trip to the Bahamas," he laughed. And seeing that Robert was really serious, Tate hesitated and then continued. "I really have all that a man could want, Robbie. Even though my wife is gone and my children are grown, I have purpose. And people I care about and who, I think, care about me."

"That's enough?" quizzed Robert.

"It's enough for me," Tate answered. "I look more to matters of the soul than possessions. When my wife died, a little of me died, too. And gradually, I found my way home again. To God." Tate stopped a moment and gave a pensive look. "You asked me what I really want? I would love to bring that to someone else who needs it."

I'd stand a better chance of giving him the car or the trip to the Bahamas, thought Robert. *I'll try to find something else for this Bible-thumper,* he resigned himself.

The next few days found Robert weakening, but not in as much pain. The patches did their job. He could rest comfortably for a few hours, get up and move around a little, and then rest a little more.

The shelter had arranged for a $10 gift certificate for every resident to spend for anything that they needed or wanted. It was just a little Christmas gift from the donations that the shelter had received; a little day brightener for people who had virtually nothing.

Robert accepted his graciously and then set out to do something he had thought about the last few days. Maybe he couldn't give Tate what he really wanted for Christmas, but he could buy him a Bible and inscribe something nice in it. Then, when Robert was gone, Tate could read it and remember him. Robert, aka Robbie, from the shelter, the one Tate gave a crap about. *He probably gave a crap about the others, too,* Robert realized, but Tate always made him feel special.

There was a used bookstore about two blocks away, and Robert scurried as much as he could to reach it before closing. It was Christmas Eve and he didn't know how long they would be open.

When he entered the shop, the clerk grimaced slightly. It was then that he knew what he must look like. Unshaven, unkempt, sickly. Maybe she thought he was there to rob the place!

"Can I help you?" she asked.

"Do you have any Bibles?" Robert replied.

"We have a few. I'll show you," the clerk answered. He could tell that she didn't want to take her eyes off of him, but was curious as to why he would want a Bible.

"This one's nice," she said, giving him a large handsomely leather bound NIV version.

He quickly turned it over to see the price. $15. Too much, but he decided to look inside for any stains or marks. The front was clear of any inscriptions so he made a counter offer. "I only have a $10 gift card," he told the clerk.

As she considered the offer, he was thrown into another coughing fit.

Watching his painful gasps for air, all she could think was to *get him out of the store!* "We're about to close, so yes, in the spirit of Christmas, $10 will be fine. Do you have the tax?"

As he started to shake his head, she quickly offered, "Never mind, the gift card will be fine." After making the quick exchange, she placed it in a Christmassy-looking sack and handed it to him. "Enjoy and Merry Christmas," the clerk said with a little smile.

He walked out of the store and noticed it was beginning to snow. He felt excitement for once. Along with that there was a feeling of, what was it? Oh. Joy! *Wow! That hasn't happened in a while*, he realized. *Doing something for someone else makes me feel good! What a kicker that is, especially for someone who's pretty much been a taker most of his life!*

His step was a bit peppier on the way back to the shelter. He could place the Bible under the tree and Tate would find it. When he opened the Bible, he would see that it was from Robert. As his happiness grew in thinking that he was giving something that Tate would surely love, Robert was caught by surprise. *Isn't that what I wanted to do*, he thought? *Amazing! I guess that I got an answer to my little prayer. Maybe God hasn't given up on me yet!* he chuckled to himself.

When he arrived back at the shelter, he was tempted to place the Bible under the tree, but there were so many people around. He really didn't want to leave it in front of everyone. There would be so many questions. Who's it for? Is it from you? Why'd you buy something for Tate? And on and on and on. So he decided to take it back to his cot.

Maybe I'll open it and see if something pops out at me, he thought. *People talk about providence all the time. Let's see if it's true,* he incredulously pondered to himself. He sat on the cot and opened the Bible to a random page. His eyes fell upon Matthew 7:11. He read, "If you, then, though you are evil, know how to give good gifts to your children, how much more will your Father in heaven give good gifts to those who ask him!" *Interesting,* he mused.

And then he read another. John 3:16. *Now here's one I know,* he remembered. "For God so loved the world that he gave his one and only Son, that whoever believes in him shall not perish but have eternal life." *Another interesting one,* he mused again.

And he continued to read until he realized that it was nearing six o'clock. Tate would soon be here telling him dinner was ready. He didn't want to give up the Bible just yet, but he would need to inscribe it soon and place it beneath the tree when no one was looking. It had to be soon so Tate could see it before he left for the night to go on vacation after Christmas. He finally settled upon an inscription and moved furtively to the tree.

When dinner had been cleared, he walked with Tate back toward the sleeping quarters. He had to make Tate see the gift so he asked, "Can we walk past the tree one more time, Tate? It's pretty safe to say that it's my last Christmas and I just want to see it as much as I can."

"Sure, Robbie," Tate answered.

As they neared the tree, Robert slowed his pace and glanced beneath the tree. Tate soon followed his line of sight and went over to the beautiful Bible situated alone on top of the tree skirt. He picked it up and opened to the first page. When he read the inscription, his eyes welled with tears.

"You're not finished reading this yet, are you, Robbie?" he asked.

"It's for you, Tate," he answered. "I couldn't give you what you wanted, but I knew that you would love this book."

Tate looked directly at Robert's face. "I think you did, son. Just reading the inscription tells me that this book has touched you, too. You bought this Bible for me, but in so doing, it called you. Indirectly, I guess, I reintroduced you to God. Thank you, Robbie."

As they walked back toward Robert's cot, Tate asked him, "Do you believe in angels, Robbie?"

"Yeah, I guess I do," he replied.

"Well, I do, too," Tate continued. "You asked me what I wanted the other night and I told you that I wanted to bring God's joy to someone else. I realized that it was really to bring God into your life. Not just someone, but you. I later prayed about it. You know, you were my angel because your gift to me brought you to God. Does that sound confusing?"

"Funny, Tate," Robert sighed. "I did a little prayer of my own to give you a gift that you would love." He smiled and then added, "I'm not as close to God as you are, or for that matter, many people, but I believe He exists. I want to know more, Tate. I haven't got much time left on earth, but for once, I'd like to know where I'm going. It's been a long time since that happened. I guess I'm my own angel, too," he laughed.

The two of them spent time that night going over passages of special comfort to those in need of spiritual hope and healing. What most comforted Robert was Romans 11:6 "And if by grace, then it is no longer by works; if it were, grace would no longer be grace." It was so simple and now Robert accepted it. He believed it.

Five days later, while still on vacation, Tate received a call from the shelter. Robert had died in his sleep, just as he had wanted. As Tate whisked away the tears that were now forming, he picked up the Bible Robert had given to him and again read the inscription.

"To Tate, but mostly to God who gave me Tate. Remember me. Love, Robbie."

CHRISTOPHER

"Hurry up, guys. We have places to go and I want to see Grandma Rachel." For just a moment, Chris caught himself by surprise. *How many times had he said just the opposite to his mother?* he wondered. "I've got to go see the kids now, Mom."

Things were always busy this time of year, but still, he missed doing some of the more important traditions shared by his family for years. There were always the Christmas preparations that started well before Thanksgiving. One herald of the season was making gingerbread creations for a holiday festival that raised money for one of the local charities.

Chris remembered how many years ago his parents used to make gingerbread houses, sell them to a confectionary and then donate the money to several charities. They also used to buy presents for needy children, donate to the Salvation Army and Pastor's Discretionary fund at their church, adopt a family or grandparent, and do many other wonderful and fulfilling activities during the season. Their traditional Christmas Eve Open House was also one of his most pleasant memories. Afterward, the family would attend midnight services. But all that had changed in recent years.

"OK, into the car, and let's go now," he said. "Shannon, I'm going to drop you and Joey off at your Grandma Anna's house. I have to be at Grandma Rachel's by 5:30 p.m. They are having their annual Christmas get-together at her place."

"Can we come?" asked Joey. Shannon already knew the answer but waited for "Daddy Chris" to give the answer.

"I'm afraid not, son," Chris replied. "This is really just for adults. But I'll take you to see Grandma soon. OK?"

The rest of the ride to their maternal Grandmother's house was fairly quiet. They loved spending time with their "Daddy" even though he wasn't their biological father, or even their legal father at that. But for all intents and purposes, and in matters of the heart, he was indeed their father. They would go anywhere with him, if they could.

Chris had been engaged to their mother for five years, when Shannon was just seven and Joey almost two. He took to them as readily as they accepted him. Since Hannah's ex-husband and their biological father really wasn't in the picture anymore, it was great to have a "daddy" around. After the engagement broke up, Hannah moved away but left the children with her parents to prevent further disruption in their lives. Chris, however, remained a constant, much to the grateful appreciation of the grandparents. In truth, he needed Shannon and Joey as much as they needed him.

Early in his relationship with women, Chris realized that he wanted a family like the one he had grown up in. His first love was more or less a secret one. And although his parents suspected that he was involved with the young lady, they were quiet on the subject of whether this would be Chris' real love in life.

When Chris later met Hannah, the entire family loved her. They also loved Shannon and Joey, and welcomed them into the family. They, too, became related "by heart" and given the honorary titles of Grandma Rachel and Grandpa Ben. When Chris and Hannah had their first big fight and pending breakup, Chris was beside himself and paced the floor. When Rachel tried to comfort him and suggested that he pray about it, he said that he had. Rachel also told him she did not know if Hannah was the one, but if so, he should do everything in his power to make it work. "Having the right person in your life is the most important thing in the world," she told him. "I thought that I was in love once before your Dad, but I am so glad now that it didn't work out. If Hannah is right, it will work out. If not, Honey, then you just have to wait. I want you to have the kind of love that your Dad and I have."

"I know, Mom," Chris confessed. "It's all I ever wanted."

So Chris grew into an exceptional young man. At twenty-nine, he still hadn't married because he hadn't found the "right one" yet. He did go out socially, but between work, spending time with the kids and his now widowed mother, as well as night school to pursue a career he had previously delayed, he didn't leave a lot of time for himself to pursue a real romantic relationship. It was also something he never knew concerned his mother. While Rachel appreciated his attentiveness, and his stepping in for his father to help her whenever he could, he never knew that she prayed for him; for him to find direction and happiness.

Chris did many things that his parents used to do. He had bought presents at Christmas time for needy children since his teens. He donated to many charities, even through the year. And he later started doing gingerbread creations, competing with his parents for the most unusual and ornate entries. After his father passed on, he collaborated with his mother on gingerbread entries to the holiday festival. "What a remarkable young man," was a common description of Chris made by family, and for that matter, by anyone else who really knew him.

"OK guys, we're here," Chris stated when they arrived at their Grandmother's house. "I'll get you inside with the presents we just bought, and then I've got to run." He gingerly grabbed the three big bags of Christmas gifts that Shannon and Joey selected during their shopping trip to the mall, and then helped the children up the steep walk to the house. "Don't slip," he cautioned.

After they opened the door to their Grandma's house, Anna came quickly to greet them. "Let me help you with those," she told Chris while taking one of the heavier sacks from him. "Come in and stay awhile. Grandpa Vic will be home soon."

"Sorry, I can't, Anna," Chris replied. "I'm headed toward my Mom's place. They're having their annual holiday gathering and I want to help her get ready."

"How is she doing, Chris?" Anna asked.

Chris thought a moment and decided to just give a brief answer that would sound a little more positive. He knew that she wasn't doing all that great, but her spirits were good and she never complained. The rheumatoid arthritis had taken its toll. She had great difficulty doing the many common things most people take for granted. She needed help getting out of bed, getting dressed, putting on makeup, and of course she could no longer prepare her own meals. That was what finally sent her to the assisted living and long-term care residence. She never seemed to mind because it was more important to her not to be a burden on her son. Chris had tried his best to prolong the inevitable by doing as much as he could for his mother, but the day had finally come when Rachel had said "enough."

"She's doing OK, but I wish she could do better," he managed to say.

Anna could tell that he responded with sadness. *What a great son*, she thought. *Rachel is lucky to have him, but what a great job of child rearing she and Ben must have done to produce such a fine young man. Why did Hannah let him get away?* she questioned again for about the hundredth time.

As soon as Shannon and Joey were settled, Chris gave them quick pecks on the cheeks, told them he loved them, and then headed off toward Pleasant Estates Assisted Living.

He parked several hundred feet from the entry because the lot appeared to be very full. There was still snow on the ground and it might be a little slick, he remembered as he grabbed the one wrapped gift from the back seat of his car. As he entered the facility, he noted that all of the Christmas decorations were up and the smell of cookies and mulled cider wafted through the air. It certainly looked festive, but it still wasn't the fond memories of his childhood, or even those from most of his adulthood. He knew that his mother must miss the same things, too.

Rounding the corner to Rachel's room, he almost bumped into Cassie, one of the nurses. "Oh, sorry," he said. "How's Mom doing?"

Recovering from a near impact, Cassie smoothed out her uniform, and said, "She's been a little down today. She caught a slight cold, and you know that a little fever always takes something out of them."

"Uh, that's too bad," Chris said. His mother never really got depressed, but when she was sick, it always hit her hard.

"She's still going to the holiday get-together, right?"

"Yes, she's going. I don't think you could stop her. She's dressed and waiting for you. And, oh, by the way, she has a gift for you, too," Cassie said as she smiled.

"OK, thanks, Cassie. I'll go see her."

Entering through the door, Chris said, "Hi, Mom!" with as much Christmas cheer as he could muster.

"Hi, Honey," Rachel replied.

He then crossed to where she was sitting and gave her a quick peck on the cheek. "This is for you," he said proudly holding out the wrapped gift for her.

"It's beautiful, son. And I have one for you as well," she said while motioning to the little table beside the bed. "Let's take them down the hall because that is where everyone is opening their gifts."

Opening gifts on Christmas Eve. First year here so I guess things will be different. Well, this is just one of many, thought Chris. *Normally, we would be spending this time at our Open House and then go to church,* but nothing else had really been normal in the years since losing his Dad anyway. Nevertheless, it was a memory that cropped up every year at this time; really, just a part of so many wonderful memories. It was hard to give them up.

"OK, ready, Mom?" he asked.

"Let's go, Honey." She smiled up at him from her wheelchair. And with that, he wheeled his mother down the hallway.

The room to the event was lavish. Rows of white poinsettia damask tablecloths filled the room, each topped with a centerpiece of greenery interspersed with silver Christmas balls and three red candles of varying height. Boughs of greenery hung from the ceiling flanked by red velvet bows, and in the corner stood a magnificent nine-foot tree. It was decorated with golden angels each bearing the name of a resident, red bows, silver balls, and crystal bells. The sound of instrumental Christmas music filled the room, directing attention to the nativity above the fireplace. It created a reverent ambience leading to the most inviting and inspiring setting that one could imagine. *What a tribute to God in all His glory!* was an immediate thought by those who entered the double glass-paned doors.

The night was electric. A choir from a nearby church sang as dinner was served, conversations were plentiful and joyous, and Chris soon forgot that he had missed the Christmas Eve service at church. *He was at church here*, he quickly thought at one time. God's presence was here just as surely as it would have been at any place of worship. Chris was reminded of the passage, "Where two or three are gathered…" *This is truly what God intended for us,* thought Chris. *The community of man, coming together to love one another and to give praise to our Father in Heaven. And to love and remember my Dad, too,* he added.

And finally, it was time to exchange gifts. Chris retrieved the one for his Mom and the one she had bought for him from the table nearest the tree.

"Here, Mom. I hope you like it," he said.

"You know that I will," Rachel replied. "Now open yours, too," she demanded with enthusiasm.

As they both unwrapped their presents, they were struck by how each had managed to find just the right gift for the other.

As tears filled her eyes, Rachel quietly said, "I love it, son. How could you have known what I really needed?" And then she held up the beautifully framed portrait that he had painted of her with her darling Ben.

"Finish opening yours now," she managed to say.

All Chris had seen initially was a travel brochure. As he continued to unwrap his present, he questioned his mother.

"Mom, how did you manage to get this for me?"

He knew that Rachel could not participate in any of the shopping excursions offered by the facility, and she no longer had a computer at her disposal to order online.

"I'll tell you in a minute, Honey. Just open it," Rachel directed.

"Oh, my God, Mom!" he exclaimed. It was an expense-paid vacation for two to an all-inclusive resort in Hawaii. He had not been there since the year before his Dad died. It was a family dream vacation, the last the three would take together.

"I thought you might like it," Rachel said with glistening eyes. "In answer to your question, I had some help. There is a new recreation coordinator. She's about your age and she helped do the research and find the best deal for me. You can go whenever you want, and take whomever you wish."

"I wish you could go with me, Mom."

"No, this is a fun getaway. Even if I could go, which we both know isn't possible, you need to go and have a great time with someone who can enjoy it with you. Oh, and you should meet Daphne. She was my little Christmas angel who helped."

Just then, Daphne walked into the room. "Sorry I'm late everybody, but I wanted to bring you something special." At that, she gestured for a stream of visitors to enter. "I brought you the cast from 'It's a Wonderful Life.' It was playing at the Community Theatre and I thought that you all might enjoy it. These wonderful people wanted to do something special this Christmas Eve and they couldn't think of any place they would rather be."

Not one person in the room could think of a more wonderful time or place to be either. They were among loved ones and the feeling of God's grace was in abundance.

Later, Rachel would introduce Chris to Daphne, who truly was her Christmas angel in more than one way. That night, neither realized that not only had Daphne helped Rachel find the perfect Christmas gift for Chris, but she would also be the fulfillment of Rachel's frequent prayer for Chris to find the kind of love she and Ben had once shared. And the best part of it all was when Chris and Daphne both had a wonderful time in Hawaii on their honeymoon.

LEAH

It was getting close to Christmas again and Leah sadly reflected on the fact that this would be her second Christmas without Steve. Steve, her husband, best friend, lover, and soul mate. The past year had been filled with "firsts": first Thanksgiving without him, first birthday without him, first anniversary without him, first Valentine's Day without him, first Easter without him. The list was endless. Now she was into the "seconds."

To make matters worse, if they could be, because of Steve's cancer and her own progressing neurological issue, she had gone on disability and retired last year. Shaking her head, Leah again thought of all that she had been through: retirement, becoming a widow, selling (or at least trying to sell) the house they had built and lived in for twenty-seven years, and recently buying another home; all this at fifty-seven years of age.

"I need something, God," she prayed. "I miss Steve so much. Please lead me where I should be. Make me useful like I felt with Steve." When such prayers occurred, and they occurred often, Leah found herself lost in thought. *What can I do?* was a common plea.

No one really knew how many times Leah cried, or rather sobbed. In truly desperate times, she found herself writing letters to Steve on the computer. That's what the grief workshop had taught her to do. And journal. Yes, write in it everyday until there was no longer a need. That she had learned at the suggestion of a very kind nurse who suggested that as therapy for the both of them. Reading Steve's journal over and over would always make Leah cry. She was still writing everyday.

"I brought you something, Baby," was a very common statement by Steve. It might have been some candy that Leah loved, or sometimes a surprise clothing item from her favorite dress shop. There was one not far from where he commuted to work as well as the one in the town in which they lived. No matter which store, if Leah was along, Steve always delighted in encouraging her to buy more. He also could pick clothes that always fit her, and were perfect to her taste. "No, she won't like that," was a statement that sales clerks learned to appreciate. He was always right.

Steve was also a romantic. Many other men in his office secretly cringed when they knew that he was buying flowers for Leah again. They felt guilty that they weren't quite as thoughtful for their own wives. On the other hand, the women in his office were in awe. But, all the women in

Leah's office were quick to acknowledge how they wished that their husbands were half as attentive and romantic. To everyone, it was obvious that Leah and Steve shared a special love. Together they were a team, and together they were whole.

When Steve lost his battle with cancer, everyone worried about Leah. "Would she be able to live on her own?" Their two sons were grown and out of the house. Although they would check on their mother, they wondered, *did she need the doting attention that Dad always gave her?* Friends and family were concerned. What people did not realize, Leah knew, is that it wasn't the things Steve did for her physically, but it was what he did emotionally that really mattered. He made her laugh and he didn't pamper her because of her illness. He made sure that she rested when needed and didn't push, but she never gave in and neither would he let her give in. With his cancer, she did the same for him. While many people would think that their recent lives read like a Greek tragedy, they refused to live their lives like one.

Thinking again of Steve, Leah remembered once when Steve turned her upset to laughter. "Steve, I can't believe that the hospital is billing us again for this. I've called the insurance company twice. I guess I'll write them a letter that they can't ignore and threaten to call the Insurance Commissioner," she ranted. It was about the fourth time he had heard this today, so he calmly took the paper from her hand, placed it on the floor, and began jumping up and down on it. When he looked at Leah's shocked expression, he said, "Now have we run it into the ground enough?" At that, she could do nothing but burst out laughing! Needless to say, the anger-filled moment was broken and she could put the matter aside until she was ready to deal with it. Steve was like that. He knew when and how to make her laugh, when to hold her if she was sad, and most of all, how to show her how much she was loved. That was a hard thing to lose. Leah once told a friend that that is "how every woman should be loved."

With Christmas approaching, Leah knew that the only way to make something of the season was to continue what she and Steve loved to do. Buying presents and doing things to serve others were what brought them the most joy. Last Christmas, Leah continued with many of their annual projects like the gingerbread creation for Big Brothers/Big Sisters. Her oldest son, Chad, helped her to complete the creation that Steve had wanted to do for their seventh project, a whimsical Noah's ark. Each year, she and Steve traded off on projects based on whatever idea the other one wanted. Steve would not see Noah's ark (or maybe he would from Heaven), but it was something they had to do. To her son and Leah's delight and surprise, it auctioned at the highest bid for the night and took one of the prizes. This, on top of the festival dedicated to Steve's memory. It was bittersweet, but lovely. Leah knew that she and Chad must continue to do the gingerbread festival.

But thinking back to other instances when she and Steve had been a team, Leah remembered so many times when they gave to the poor, adopted a grandparent from the senior center, found just the right presents for their sons, gave to the Pastor's Discretionary Fund, and gave many other quiet and anonymous gifts to help others. She tried to do that last year, too. It was a way to honor Steve, and it kept him close to her.

Of course, finding the right gifts to delight each other was another wonderful experience of the season, but unfortunately, that was one that couldn't be continued. Giving to others, that was the true joy of Christmas, and at least, that part could be continued.

Leah had had a successful career until early retirement. The stress of Steve's cancer and her worsening disability just made working impossible. She didn't miss her job for the three months that she traveled extensively with Steve as they tried various treatments. But as each failed and they had come to the end of the trials, Leah's exhaustion could not be a part of it. She could not give in to it until it could no longer affect her being with Steve. Nothing would take her from his side.

This last year after losing him she was learning how to cope with living alone, how to do things on her own when joint decisions had always been the norm, and how to fill a void so deep that no chasm could compare. Yes, Leah's prayer was always the same. She needed something to be whole again, if only for a little while.

So on this day of remembering and Christmas approaching, she asked herself again, "What can I do?" *I do love to write, but I also love to help people. I wouldn't mind earning a little extra next year,* she grimaced. Steve had provided well for her, but still, not having to rely so much on life insurance proceeds would be a real plus. And it occurred to her. *I can write comfort.* And indeed she could. *Wouldn't that be funny?* she mused. *The Assistant Professor who thought I wrote verbosely my sophomore year in college, but loved Faulkner, would faint if I really, actually wrote a book! And I can write more like my favorite authors,*

Michael Creighton, John Grisham, Dan Brown, Janet Evanovich. They are readable and you don't get bogged down in their literary style. Take that, Professor Whatever your name was! But write what?

As Leah tried to remember what gave her the most comfort, she suddenly felt the urge to write about things of the heart. "Write about something you know," was a common statement from her father. A lawyer, he was an excellent writer who unfortunately spent more time writing legal documents than using his gift of prose to entertain. What he did, however, was to produce one daughter who was a freelance writer, and now this one who wished to write.

And just as suddenly as the idea occurred to Leah, so did the "how." She sat at the computer and began writing. The words flowed and it was surprisingly easy. When she had finished the first few chapters, she realized how much pleasure and comfort there was for her in this task, and how much divinity there was also. The ideas, the peace and comfort with which the stories ended, the creativity, all had an origin outside of herself. She realized that God was truly working through her and she must share her work. That was the hard part.

She admired and understood why it took so many years for her writer-sister to actually submit and professionally begin her career. Leah realized that your words are your thoughts, and they are a link to your soul. It is hard to be that vulnerable, but she decided to play it safely. She would first send the initial chapters to another sister and see what she thought. When the email came back that it made her sister cry, and she loved it, and all the other people who read it loved it, that was more than Leah hoped for. *Wait. Other people?* Leah thought with a panic. And then her sister called.

"You've got to do something with this, Leah," her sister gushed. "It's too good. Keep writing."

Leah wanted very much to also share this with her writer-sister, but was very apprehensive, too. Her sister was a professional and her opinion would carry a lot of weight. That also might be the determining factor of where this goes. *I know that I have to test the waters,* she thought. In fact, she sat down at the computer again and wrote for three hours on a chapter that would have special meaning for that sister.

Before sending her manuscript, still in progress, Leah told her sister that she would send it only if her sister promised to provide honest feedback, either positive or negative. For almost twenty-four hours, Leah waited for her sister's comments. *Would she like the story that I wrote for her? Would she like the premise of angelic interventions? Would she think it was worthy of going further?* And then the e-mail arrived. Her sister had loved all of the stories, and she was so moved in reading her own that she cried twice while doing so. Now it was settled. Leah had to find a way to bring the book to fruition.

Her next-door neighbor was a published author and former journalist. He had an agent and also had a friend who had self-published. He agreed to serve as an initial editor.

As Leah reflected on this process of writing a book that was capable of touching others and bringing comfort in the season, she realized that God had answered her frequent prayer: Steve had been her Christmas angel. He was the muse. Without him, there would have been no desire for comfort or to lessen her pain by lessening that of others. God had put Steve into her life for many things as well as being the inspiration for this book. And this, dear reader, is my story. My middle name is Leah.

CONCLUSION

God hears our prayers. He can use ethereal angels to answer them, as well as assign an angelic task to one of us. It can be as simple as a kind word or maybe just a random act of kindness. But, what an incredible opportunity we are given to make this world a little better place! And it can come so unexpectedly, too.

God knows our hearts and what we really need. And sometimes, it is just to be needed. That is when, I think, He allows us to be "angels on earth" and we are given the wisdom to realize that the mature heart finds fulfillment and peace not in possessions or aspirations, but in matters of the soul.

ACKNOWLEDGMENTS

Many thanks to my family and friends for giving me feedback and encouragement; to my author-friend, Stan Hamilton, who helped me to polish my original manuscript; to my editor, Sarah Kennington, who provided a wealth of direction and support; to Jennifer M. Blackwell-Yale for her copyediting skills and patience with my own edits; and to the presence of God in my life that inspired this message of care and comfort.

ABOUT THE AUTHOR

 A graduate of The University of Kansas, Vicki Julian has spent most of her adult life writing in the business world while working in the field of early childhood and a government call center. She honed her story telling abilities as a preschool director and Sunday school teacher. Her first book is from the heart to bring comfort and inspiration to others.

Recently retired, Vicki resides in Kansas near her two adult sons. She remains active in her church and is a supporter of many local charitable efforts.